I0547191

Witch

Curse of the Hybrids

Book 4

LISA LAGALY

PUBLISHING

Published in the United States of America

First Printing, 2025

ISBN

ebook: 978-1-966455-11-0
paperback: 978-1-966455-10-3

LL Publishing
Lisa1.author@gmail.com

Prologue

MARCH

Honey sat next to her friend Walter in the chairs in front of her cousin's desk. Zavier tapped on his keyboard a few times then turned the big screen to face them. A map was displayed with a rectangular-like shape outlined in the middle of it.

"I've been looking into different properties," Zavier said. "This one is the most promising. It's over 200 acres, butts up against one of the highways into the park, and is at least five times cheaper than anything else I can find. The original homestead is basically inaccessible on all but one side due to the surrounding cliffs, so it would be easy to defend, but there's a catch."

"What is it?" Walter asked.

"It's cursed. The moment someone buys the place, everything starts going wrong. Sometimes it's as simple as two flat tires and sometimes it's as awful as losing every cent they have. If they're stubborn, eventually the buyer does lose every cent they have."

"Who owns it then?" Honey asked.

"A horse."

"What!?" she and Walter said at the same time.

"It's the only way the bank could have some control over it without being ruined. The curse doesn't apply to animals. The last owner was the bank manager's cat. Unfortunately, the curse is smart enough to recognize that cats and horses can't possibly be managing humans, so the bank can't do anything with the land. It just sits there. Occasionally, the bank finds a sucker and make a couple of thousand, then the owner defaults and the bank gets the land again. I'm very glad you're here, Honey. I know it's a long shot and I don't expect it will work, but I'd like you to take a look at the place."

"Zavier I don't think I'll be able to do anything. You should ask a witch or the witch council."

"I did. The bank has contacted them multiple times. They can't do it. The former owner of the property was a powerful witch himself. He spent years preparing the curse to ensure that the land would always be in his family. Unfortunately, he should have spent more time taking care of his finances and raising children. He only had one son and his son didn't have any children. He died over 120 years ago."

"That's sad," she said.

"From all accounts, his son wasn't a very nice man."

"If it's a written curse, all you have to do is destroy the original writing," she supplied, although she doubted it would be that easy.

"It's not written anywhere. The story is that when the bank came to take the property, Mr. Witthem met them at the gate with a crow and started speaking in the devil's tongue. He then slaughtered the crow and dribbled its blood in a line all around his property. There's a cartoon of it in an old newspaper."

"There couldn't possibly be enough blood in one crow to go around 200 acres of land," Walter scoffed.

"You're right," Zavier nodded. "If he did use blood, he probably had the line mostly drawn with other animals before the bankers got there."

All Honey knew of curses came from one book and what the librarian had told her. The part on blood curses had been short and dire.

"Blood curses are bad. The only way to break a blood curse is with more blood, but it has to be more precious than what was originally used. If it was animal blood, then you'd have to sacrifice a human and if it was human blood, you'd have to sacrifice yourself and if someone sacrificed themselves in the first place, that's pretty much unbreakable."

"Unless you can find a curse breaker," Zavier said, looking at her expectantly, "which unfortunately are very, very rare, so rare there hasn't been one in over a hundred years, or so the council told me."

Just because she had been able to fix his head after he'd drunk that spelled beer didn't mean she was a curse breaker but, "I suppose it can't hurt to look."

1

KIDNAPPED

Flames and smoke surrounded her. She couldn't see anything but her mother lying at her feet, reaching toward her, asking for help. She tried. For at least the hundredth time Honey desperately pulled air from the flames and tried to freeze the fire, but no matter what she did, the flames always won.

"Wake up!"

Icy cold liquid drenched Honey's face and shirt. The heat and smoke and awful smell were abruptly gone, replaced by the much friendlier scents of old cement, dust, and spring grass.

It was a dream? It had felt so real.

Something sharp tapped her cheek. "Come on, open those eyes."

She opened one eye and then the other. Unable to fully see due to the water and the crustiness left by the tears she'd shed while she was dreaming, and unable to move her arms for some reason, she scrunched her eyes closed and back open a few times. The back of her neck was sore, probably because she had been sleeping while sitting upright, but why were her shoulders so stiff and uncomfortable? She tried to move them, then realized it wasn't because of how she slept. Her arms were bound behind the chair she was sitting in. A tall man with dark clothes, dark hair just starting to turn silver at the temples, and a child's faded, red plastic bucket smirked down at her. She'd seen him before, but she couldn't remember where or when. She couldn't remember much of anything. Her mind felt hazy and numb.

"At last, Honey Smith, we meet."

"Who are you? Where is my mom?"

Without taking his eyes off of her, he tossed the bucket toward the dark corner behind him. It looked like they were in a shed or perhaps an old detached garage. The floor was as brown as dirt, or maybe it *was* dirt. Cinder block walls were topped by an open ceiling that was so aged, the wood that made up the underside of the roof was stained almost black. She couldn't see any windows, but natural-looking light was coming in from somewhere because they weren't in total darkness.

"You don't remember?"

Like magic, memories started playing through her mind. Her mom and dad were gone, burned in a fire. She'd run and had been captured by a wolf pack who didn't realize she was also half witch. The Luna of the pack had sent her to college because of her outstanding SAT score where she'd met her best friends – four freshman boys who'd basically adopted her after she stole their pizza. She'd won an MMA tournament and rescued a cousin she didn't know she had. He was now an alpha to a pack of abused women and children and wanted her to break a curse on some land. He believed she was the first curse breaker to be born in centuries, but other people would kill her if they found her because she was a hybrid and hybrids were cursed and just knowing about them made other people cursed. She'd told her four friends what she was before she knew that, unfortunately, but so far, they seemed fine. Her cousin Zavier and Alpha Silver, who had turned out to be her biological father instead of her uncle, also knew, but that was it.

Her parents were gone. The fire had been real.

"I am your father, or I should have been, if your mother hadn't turned out to be a slut."

A vision of a guy in a big black plastic helmet and a cape floated through her brain with her other memories. Where had that come from? She shook it away.

Now she remembered the guy in front of her. He was the man who'd been in the witch library with her grandmother and great-grandmother when they'd discovered her mom had died but that there was a child: her.

"What do you want with me?"

He grabbed her chin and turned her face from one side to the other. "Well, that depends. What kind of magic do you have?"

"I'm a wolf."

He released her chin and stepped toward a long table that was pushed up against one wall. "Not according to this." He whipped around and shoved a familiar guitar-pick shaped piece of plastic in front of her nose. She'd first seen one like it in Texas when a girl with blue hair – no, she'd had the blue hair – the girl had normal hair and had wanted to test her blood to see what blood line she

8

came from. Honey had melted the test before it could reveal what she was, but this one had two holes burned at the end of two of the lines. "You are both witch and wolf – a monster."

He'd taken her blood while she was unconscious, the jerk. "I'm not a monster."

"You don't look like one. I'm surprised. I was wondering how you were able to hide yourself so easily. Your mother must have fixed you when you were born. Can you transform into a wolf?"

"I just told you I was a wolf."

"You are only half-wolf. Didn't you get any powers from your mother?"

Deny, deny, her dad had taught her. Make people doubt themselves. "Why do you think my mother was a witch?"

He abruptly lunged at her and slapped her face. She'd been punched and kicked many times during her MMA bouts, but somehow his slap was more painful that a lot of those punches.

He smirked at her. "Now, what power did you get from your mother?"

"Wolf ones."

He slapped her again, but she was ready this time. She froze her cheek. She didn't know if he could tell. When she froze people their skin didn't become cold, it just put everything on hold and locked it into place. Theoretically, unless he hit her very hard, her skin wouldn't bruise and she wouldn't feel pain because her nerve endings wouldn't fire. Her head turned a little from his blow because she hadn't frozen her neck, but her cheek didn't hurt. She slowly turned her head to face him and gave him the most unimpressed look she could muster.

His nostrils flared. His hand was behind his back, but she could tell by the way his arm wiggled that he was shaking it. Ha. He'd hurt himself and she'd gotten a good whiff of his chest. Based on the metallic smell, there were several shield charms under the thin fabric of his shirt. That would make it difficult to freeze him, but it also suggested he tended to rely on magic. He wouldn't be expecting a physical fight.

He lunged at her again, this time going for her hair. She moved faster than him and turned her head to bite his hand with her human teeth. She didn't want him to know how fast she could transform, not yet. She tugged enough to get the message across and tear his skin a little before she let go. His blood had a tint of hot asphalt – a fire witch. Huh, she hadn't realized she could taste magical talents. She spit the blood to the side while keeping an eye on him in case he tried to attack again.

Biting him might have earned her a small reprieve. He was cradling and inspecting his hand like she'd broken it.

"You bit me!"

"I was defending myself."

"You truly are a monster."

She knew what he was going to do as soon as he lifted his hands. According to her mom, magical fire needed oxygen or an oxidant just as much as normal fires. Some people were strong enough that they could conjure up the required oxygen, but usually there was enough around they didn't need to. She quickly pulled all the air from around

10

his hands before he could let loose. A flame sputtered in his palms, but that was as far as it went.

He looked at his palms, gave a decent growl for a witch, and tried again. He was one of those powerful conjurers, because this time flames shot toward her. She sent a strong wind in his direction and threw herself backwards. Her chair cracked promisingly but didn't break. So much for *that* Black Widow move. Now she was confined, on her back, and there was still a crazy man threatening her with flaming hands.

Wasn't there?

Ah, no. The crazy guy was frantically patting at his smoking clothes. Her wind must have pushed the flames back at him. You'd think a fire mage would wear fire-proof clothing.

She took advantage of his distraction and quickly transformed to a wolf, then back again while holding her hands apart and her feet away from the bottom of the chair. The tape that had held her hands together and her ankles down reappeared on her limbs, but her hands and ankles were no longer connected. She rolled out of the chair and quickly scanned the part of the room she hadn't been able to see. She was right, it was an old garage. There was another long table in front of a door big enough for a car. Above it was the source of the light – a small, square, dirty window. A much smaller door was to her right, just beside heavy-looking wooden shelves that ran along the other wall.

Her captor was still distracted by his smoking chest. She sprinted for the door. The handle was one of those simple ones, with a lever for thumbs. It should have been easy to open, but nothing happened when she pushed down. The door wouldn't budge when she pushed or pulled it either.

"Looking for these?" an irritating voice singsonged behind her. She glanced back to see her captor shaking a set of skeleton keys at her. "You didn't really think you'd escape that easily, did you?"

She sped up her molecules and grabbed the keys and was back to the door before he realized what she'd done. The key didn't fit. She should have known it was trick. By the time she'd figured that out, he'd pull out one of his necklaces and was muttering a spell. She smelled rope. He was trying to bind her or her powers. Not happening. She charged him before he could finish saying the words and planted her fist solidly on the sweet spot her dad had taught her when she was three.

The pansy collapsed like one of those fan-inflated air tube creatures you see in front of car dealers when the wind knocks them down. She tore through the three protection charms he was wearing, froze him, then squatted and lifted a ridiculous number of chains and cords arrayed around his skinny neck over his heavy head. There were at least ten, all with one or more charms. He was like one of those tween-aged girls pictured on necklace-crafting kits. Did that mean he also – yes, he did. She pulled three charmed bracelets off his left wrist and, fortifying herself by scrunching up her face, jammed her hand into his pocket to empty them of the charms she sensed there too.

The close stench of his burnt clothes, particularly after her horrible dreams, made her want to gag. Underneath that though, she could smell something else, something she'd smelled months ago. It reminded her a little of bergamot, a flavoring in one of the teas her mom liked. It was also the same smell she'd just spent a lifetime smelling while she watched her parents burn over and over.

"You murdered my parents."

His pale face didn't twitch. Of course it couldn't, since he was frozen and knocked unconscious, but still. She'd felt guilty about disabling his shield charms, but now?

"Why did you kill them?"

She was pretty sure he hadn't known she existed then.

God said forgive. How was she supposed to forgive someone who'd taken the two people most precious to her in the entire world? They'd had years and years left to live and he'd taken those too.

Could she be wrong?

She wasn't. There was no one else who made sense. He was a fire witch and she'd smelled him there. He had a motive too, her mom had dumped him for her dad. The man probably hated her. Unfortunately, she couldn't turn him in. First, she had no proof, and second, he'd tell everyone what she was. He'd probably be rewarded and she, she'd be executed.

The least he could do was provide her with some money and a phone so she could call her friends. She continued her search of his pockets and found a thick wallet, a decent-looking phone, more charms – how many charms did a single guy need – but no keys. She discovered his name was Gaian Graves, he was two years older than her mom, and he hadn't cleaned out his wallet in years. Instead of cash, it was full of expired credit cards and ancient tattered business cards. He even had an old faded picture of her mom in the slot facing his driver's license.

She took it.

He moaned. She froze him again. She should run, but if she did she might never know the truth for sure. She grabbed the gray tape sitting on the table and taped his hands and his feet together. Just to be safe, she put all the chains she'd removed from his neck and the things she'd emptied from his pockets on the shelves, well out of his reach, then removed the fat ring on his index finger. He wasn't wearing a watch.

It took him a few minutes to fully wake after her magic wore off. She was sitting backwards in the chair far enough away that if he lunged at her she could easily dodge. It was rather amusing to watch while he slowly realized his predicament. Like she expected, he immediately started trying to figure out how to remove the tape that bound him. She made a big production of carefully setting a stone she'd found in the corner on the floor while she froze the muscles in his limbs. It wasn't as easy as freezing a person whole, but Dad had insisted she learn because people can't talk to you when their insides were frozen.

"Where did you find that?" he demanded.

Oops, maybe he didn't own a freeze stone. She should have thought of that. She gave him a wicked smile and hoped he'd think she had it on her.

"Have you ever killed anyone, Mr. Graves?"

She'd thought about starting off with why he'd killed her mother, but then he'd know for sure who she was.

"Is that your plan? You're going to kill me?" he snarled.

She tilted her head and tried to look scary-crazy. "Should I? Are you a murderer?"

He glared at her. "Of course not."

He said it smoothly, but even her weak wolf nose could tell he was lying.

"How many people have you killed?"

"None."

"Or order killed?"

His muscles were still frozen, but by the strained look on his face and the little grunts he was making, he was trying hard to move. She didn't think he could call up a fire with his molecules frozen, but she froze his hands again just to be make sure none of his molecules had come loose.

She lifted the wallet from her lap and opened it to her mother's picture. "Who is this woman?"

"Stop playing dumb. You know who that is. You look just like her."

"Who is she to you?" Honey amended.

"My fiancé, the love of my life, the woman I waited sixteen years for. Your mother," he spat.

Part of what he said was true.

"I know you didn't love her. Why did you wait? You could have found another woman to be your wife. You aren't bad looking and you aren't *that* old. You could probably still find another woman."

"Do you know who your mother was?"

15

His shoulder twitched. She froze his muscles again. She wasn't worried about how many times she froze limbs. They recovered a lot faster than brains.

"She was a Wixx," he continued. "The last of one of the most powerful branches of the founders."

"There are lots of Wixx witches." She'd seen how many times the name popped up in the library. She had to have hundreds of distant cousins.

"They are weak offshoots with diluted bloodlines. Madeline's line was strong."

"Are you saying the Wixx line intermarried?"

"No. They kept the line strong by marrying only the strongest from other families, people like me."

"It was an arranged marriage." Her dad had mentioned it in his letter.

"Yes."

"You didn't love her. You barely knew her."

He sent another glare her way. "Just because it was arranged doesn't mean I didn't have feelings for her."

A dark smell – anger – was rolling from him. It was stronger than anything she'd ever sensed off Brayton, even before they'd become friends.

"Why are you so mad?"

"Because she let herself be sullied with the likes of your father!" he yelled.

Now they were getting somewhere. "My father? How do you know my father?"

"I saw her, them, together. They were embracing. She let a wolf touch her."

"You saw them together? Where?" Her parents were very careful of PDA. Other witches and wolves wouldn't be able to detect her mom was a witch unless she did magic, but even a human and a wolf couple was something other witches and wolves would notice.

"I followed her from the store. I just wanted to say hello. I was about to get out of my car and knock on the door when a wolf drove up on his motorcycle and right into the garage like he lived there."

That was impossible. Her dad didn't have a door opener and it was a one-car garage. "How did you know he was a wolf if you were in your car?"

He ignored her question and continued. "I walked around the house to find a window in case she needed help."

In other words, he was peeping. He must have been standing close enough when Dad drove up that he could feel her dad's wolf aura.

"He had her up against a wall. I thought he was attacking her."

"You saw them doing *what?*" She'd never even seen them kiss, just hug.

"I broke through the window and used a charm on him to get him off her. She didn't even thank me. She dropped down beside him and started touching him, calling for him. She was crying when she looked up at me. Crying, over a wolf! 'What did you do?', she asked me. I told her I'd saved her. She shook her head and told me I'd destroyed her, and it made me mad. I waited sixteen years for her and the whole time she was hiding out with a wolf, someone who wasn't even fit to breathe the same air she did, much less touch her."

The air around him shimmered with power. He was going to set himself on fire if he wasn't careful. She froze his muscles again. When that didn't work, she froze the rest of him. The shimmer faded and vanished.

She released the breath she hadn't realized she was holding, but it didn't stop the tremor in her hands or the sick feeling in her stomach. It was dumb bad luck that her parents had died. Mom must have gone shopping after she dropped her off at school. She'd probably known her dad was coming by. She always seemed to know somehow. Maybe she'd planned a nice lunch for them. Her dad had been gone for weeks. It would have been the first time they'd been alone without her around somewhere near in years.

She was glad they were truly attracted to each other. After reading her dad's letter, she'd wondered if her parents were just friends and he'd only stuck around for her.

And now they were gone.

She quickly wiped her face. Now wasn't the time to cry. She had to escape before her mom's ex woke up, but how? She hadn't found a single key on his person and the only ways out that weren't blocked were the door and the window, if she could get up to it. Maybe he'd set the key on one of the tables or the shelf? She counted in her head while checking all the surfaces and anything that looked like it had been recently disturbed. At twenty-five, she froze him again.

She didn't find a key, but she did find the blood test and a CD-like disk that had a drop of blood in the middle. It was divided into 8 wedges, each with a different symbol.

Two of the wedges had gold discoloration over the silver starting from the middle of the CD. She vaguely remembered seeing the symbols before, but she didn't recall what they meant. She stuffed both tests into her pocket.

Maybe she was looking for the wrong thing. She switched to her magical sight and searched the door for spells. Bingo. The doorknob had a faint glow that smelled like…ink. Why would a spell smell like ink? Did she have to write something? Maybe her captor traced a password in the air to get out. She hoped not. She'd never get out of here. What else could you use ink for? Drawing, coloring, printing, finger printing! She needed his fingerprints.

He was bigger than her, but he wasn't fat, far from it. She grabbed his ankles and dragged him to the door. His right hand didn't work, but putting his left hand on the handle like he was going to open the door did. She maneuvered a stone near the door into place to keep the door from shutting, then dragged him clear.

She wasn't a thief, but if she didn't eat soon, things would get dicey. Plus, Gaian had kidnapped her and transported her against her will, not to mention, murdered her parents. She felt completely justified in transferring the thirty dollars in his wallet to her pocket. It wasn't nearly enough to get her home though. According to his phone, which she unlocked with his finger, she was in rural Illinois, about 150 miles away from college and her friends. Phooey. It would take days to get home by foot. If only she'd memorized the guys' numbers instead of Alpha Silver's real one. In hindsight, she should have memorized the number of someone a little less conspicuous like

Brayton. It would make sense if she called him, since he was her alpha's son, or better, his dad. Using Gaian's phone to call an alpha that she'd barely associated with might make Gaian curious and if he found out Alpha Silver was actually her biological father rather than her uncle, it could have deadly consequences.

His finger twitched when she tossed the phone on his chest. Her time was up. She froze him one last time and slipped out the door, taking all his charms with her. She wouldn't use them, but that didn't mean he should be allowed to keep them either.

2

COVENSTEAD

Outside, the day smelled new and fresh and awash in magic, literally. Her nose twitched at the rich magical smell even as her eyes told her everything was normal. Where was the smell coming from? Long shadows stretched across the expanse of lawn in front of her thanks to the rising sun at her back. To her right was a large, two-story house, brick, with a long covered porch. Sturdy stone molding lined the windows and roof line. It was more than big enough for a family or three to live in. The only thing that stood between her and the porch was a tree trunk, but there was no one on the porch or the yard to notice her.

Not a road was in sight. The map on the phone had indicated she was in the country somewhere and this homestead was an island along a rural road in the midst of miles of farmland. If she jogged about seven miles north and west, there was a fast-food restaurant that should be open where she could eat and hopefully borrow a phone. All she had to do was find a road and get there without being seen.

She peeked around the corner of the front of the garage, expecting a long driveway and maybe a barn.

Instead, she saw what was basically a small town. Was this a covenstead? That would explain the magical smell. She'd wanted to visit one ever since her college roommate had told her about them, but Honey never thought she'd get the chance. Unless she wore a thick air shield, witches could sense her wolf side and no witch would allow a wolf into their territory. It would be like wolves letting a witch onto their pack lands.

At least ten houses of different sizes and styles and mailboxes sat side-by-side along a lengthy, gravel two-lane driveway. A median strip with shady trees and colorful flowers culminated at an equally colorful circle with a flagpole in front of the big house where the road made a loop. More flowering plants lined the small yards and gravel driveways populated with mostly older cars. It looked like a nice place to live. Not surprisingly, there were people out and about. In her quick glance, she spotted one on a porch drinking coffee, one in her yard, and a third talking through the screen door to someone in her house. Honey pulled back out of sight. They were such close neighbors, they had to know Gaian. Did they know what he was up to? Would they help her even though she was a wolf?

She couldn't take the chance.

Sliding to the other end of the wall, she peeked around the corner to the back of the garage. The houses had a normal allotment of sheds and garages, but instead of individual yards surrounded by fences, the houses shared a huge backyard that flowed downhill to a large garden and a big pond. A man with a fishing pole and a white, curly-haired dog were strolling down a well-worn path toward

22

the pond. She ducked back beside the garage before the dog turned his head. Phooey. She was running out of time. She had to go somewhere before her parent's murderer woke up and freed himself.

A large, nicely mowed yard of green stretched out in front of her. Beyond that was a solid wood fence, a line of trees, and a field. If she could just get over the fence, there was a good chance she'd be able to slip around the covenstead without being seen and then she could go north. She took one last look around to make sure it was clear, then sprinted across the grass. The fence got taller and the pickets sharper-looking as she moved closer, but it was still shorter than what they'd crawled over in WOLF class. She'd have no problems getting over. The fence was tall enough though, that she'd be jumping blind. Normally that wouldn't worry her, but if she landed in a hole and twisted her ankle, there weren't any doctors to help her here. She veered toward a flower bed and a big tree with a sturdy branch that extended over the fence.

The flower bed was a lot larger than it looked from a distance. Some of the plants were tall enough to hide someone if they crouched down, as Honey quickly discovered. She made a split-second adjustment to avoid the woman with a big hat who was pulling weeds behind a bush but still managed to leap over the area the woman was tending to, springboard off the nearby wheelbarrow, and jump high enough to pull herself onto the sturdy branch she'd aimed for.

"You'll want to watch out for the wards, dear," the lady commented while Honey worked her way around the trunk toward the fence.

Honey paused and looked down. All she could see was the top of the woman's hat and her floral gloves wrapped around the stem of the stubborn vine she was trying to pull. "You're trapped in here?"

"Of course not. The driveway is open."

Not helpful. Even if she did make it down the drive, there was no way she could outrun a car, or several.

She'd already figured out there was a ward. The magical smell of iron and lightning she'd noticed when she stepped out of the garage had gotten stronger the closer she came to the fence. She was close enough now that she could see a slight yellow glow even before she looked at it with magic. How had she not seen it from the garage? Maybe that was part of the spell.

With her magic sight, the ward looked like a very large glowing net with bright strips of yellow magic and molecules loosely woven together. The big, continuous net followed the fence all the way around the yard and as far as she could see back around the garage and the houses. While she was scoping out the extent of the net, she noticed the garage door from which she'd escaped fly open. Mom's ex was awake. Either she'd have to find a hiding place, break through the ward, or make a run for the drive.

The women beneath the tree scratched vigorously at the ground with a little hand rake. If she was a witch, Honey was certain the woman would sense she was a wolf. Why was the woman not trying to alert anyone and why had she warned Honey about the ward? Did she expect her to give up and run for the drive? Were there guards?

No one would expect her to go through the ward. Through the ward it was then, but first, Honey pulled up her air shield. There was no point in letting the woman know she had magic too.

Moving the strands turned out to be easy. Making them stay where she put them took a little finessing, but before the murderer even thought to head across the yard, she had a nice open hole carved out above the branch that was too high to crawl through and too low to step through. Oops. It was about perfect for her wolf to dive through, but she had a feeling the lady below her was watching even though she wasn't looking. Had she ever seen a wolf transform? Would she know there was something odd about her transformation? Honey decided it would be safer to stay human and dive and roll like she'd done many times on a beam in gymnastics.

"I can bury those charms for you if you want," the lady said. "He won't think to look here. He'll think you took them with you."

"Um, thank you." She'd been wondering how she was going to get them through the hole in human form. Her pockets were bulging to the point the charms were in danger of spilling out and if she put them around her neck, they might fall out of her shirt while she was diving, not that she wanted to wear anything her parents' murderer had worn. It wasn't like she'd been planning on using them anyway. She had only took them so he wouldn't have anything to protect himself with if he came after her again.

"Just drop them."

"How did you know I had them?" Had the woman sensed them? Was she planning on using them against her? They weren't all protection charms. Some of them felt quite…dangerous.

"If you don't drop them, when you dive, they'll fly out and set off the alarm."

Was the woman a mind-reader? In any case, if all went well, Honey would be outside the ward and out of reach before the woman could activate one of the charms. Fine.

She made her air shield as thick as she could, just in case she hit the ward, then, right before she dove, she dropped the charms.

The branch was wider than a balance beam, but round and rough. The dive and the roll worked, but the smaller branch poking up from the large one near the end of her roll didn't survive. Her foot knocked it off with a loud crack, sending it spinning through the air. To Honey's shock, the moment the stick touched the ground, a circle of rusty metal teeth sprang from the ground and clamped around it, snapping it in two.

A bear trap? How long had it been there? Did the witches know it was there?

"You'll want to watch out for the traps," the woman called through the fence. "There aren't any in the field."

"Thanks."

"Oh, and you may want to disable the magical tracker you've got on you."

"Thanks again. Why are you helping me?"

"Because you are the underdog. I always root for the underdog."

Did the woman mean for her words to have a double meaning? Whatever. It was nice of her to warn about the tracker – Honey hadn't even considered that. Now how to get rid of it?

She didn't smell anything until she did a full shake of her head, then she caught a faint hint of smoke. If she wasn't aware there was a tracker, she would have thought she was smelling the smoke from someone's chimney. She quickly sniffed her arms – it wasn't there. It must be on her back. She searched the molecules on and around her for anything odd. There it was, on the back of her head. The molecules flickered like a mini flame or a signal fire, which made perfect sense for a fire maker. She pulled the molecules forming the tracker apart and forced them to disperse into the air. The smoke smell disappeared.

Now how to avoid the traps? She only had to go about twenty feet to get out of the trees but there were no branches close by she could jump to, and the traps had been there so long, they were well camouflaged with old leaves. What she needed was a big stick.

The tree she was in had larger branches, but they were all too short or crooked to help. Instead, she broke off three little twigs and threw them where she was planning to dismount from her branch. Nothing happened. She carefully lowered herself into the spot, picked the sticks up, and threw them again. She did it three times before she finally reached a nice long stick. By then she didn't need it. It was clear by the way the leaves clustered unnaturally to hide the next trap that there was something odd, not to mention, the spell that made them cluster smelled like glue. Witches must really think wolves were dumb. A few feet later, she smelled a combination of rotten eggs and skunk – a repulsion spell. That explained why no one had sued the witches for using bear traps.

Holding her nose, she peeked out from the trees. Just beyond them, a barbed-wire fence separated the green space along the trees from the more organized green of an immature field of wheat. The wheat was already tall enough that she would be able hide in her wolf form if she ducked down. She stuck her head out a little farther and looked both ways. No one in sight. Just in case there was another ward waiting for her and hidden by the skunk smell, she poked her stick over the fence. Nothing happened. Tossing the stick aside, she transformed, leapt the fence, and ran.

3

OLD WOMAN WITH A CAR

It was the perfect morning for a run, especially in wolf form. It would have been even better if she wasn't running for her life.

She kept to the fields and made sure no one was coming when she crossed the roads. After four country roads, aka miles, she still hadn't seen anyone on the roads, nor had she come close to any other houses. Had she gotten away so easily?

The next field offered only short stubble to hide behind, but there was a creek running through the middle deep enough to provide cover. She jogged along it across the field, then realized it was flowing directly toward a cluster of four houses. With the trees though and the cows, she doubted anyone would notice her small, red wolf form.

Something noticed. When she neared the first house, what sounded like a hundred dogs started howling and barking and making her more scared than she'd ever felt when facing a human. At least ten hounds of different sizes and colors, most big, charged around the house toward her. She stopped following the winding creek and sprinted for the road. With luck, the creek would slow the dogs down and they'd stay on their side of the fence once she reached the road. She only had to get to the fence and jump it.

The creek slowed the dogs down about as much as it did her, that is, not at all. They were gaining when she remembered she wasn't just a wolf. She froze them. The sudden cessation of noise was startling. Someone would have noticed that. She sprinted to the fence and jumped over, then crouched beneath a bridge and transformed back into her human form. Praying the dogs would leave her alone since she was now on the road and no longer looked or smelled like a wolf, thanks to her air shield, she unfroze them. If anyone was checking on the beasts, they might notice the dogs had looked like statues for a few seconds, but would hopefully chalk it up to their imagination.

The dogs were clearly suspicious when she emerged from under the bridge and climbed up to the road. They charged the barbed-wire fence, letting her know in no uncertain terms that they did not appreciate her foray into their territory and if they ever saw her again, they'd tear her apart limb by limb. That was her interpretation anyway. She was just glad they decided to stop at the fence.

"Honey, wait."

An old woman stepped into the light from beneath a shade tree on the other side of the bridge. Honey had been so concerned about the dogs she hadn't looked carefully at the road.

"Shut up you mongrels!" the woman yelled at them, then turned to Honey with her palms up. "Not you dear. Never you. I'm your grandmother. I just want to talk. Ride with me?"

"My mom taught me never to go anywhere with strangers."

"Did she? I'm sure she did. Your mom was a smart girl. I'd offer to walk with you, but it will be safer in the car. They'll be after you."

"Why are you here?" Had she been waiting on her? That wasn't suspicious at all.

"I was waiting on you. I have a friend who sometimes sees bits of the future. She saw you here."

Oh, so that woman wasn't a mind reader.

"Does she like to garden and wear a big hat?"

Her grandma chuckled. "Sometimes. Please, I want to get to know you. I promise I won't hurt you. We can go somewhere and eat."

"Are you offering me candy?"

The woman gaped at her for a second, then said carefully, "If that's what you want."

"It was a joke Grandma. You know, because strangers offer kids candy to get into their van."

Honey recognized her from the library. She was the friendly-looking older lady, not the stern one who was her great-grandmother.

"I'm not…you believe me?"

"Yeah. I know who you are."

Tears had already started streaming down the woman's cheeks. Honey walked up to her and hugged her. Her mom had never spoken badly of her mother. Truthfully, her mom never said anything bad about anybody in her family, but Honey had always felt Mom missed her mom the most.

"Let me look at you," her grandma said after they'd both shed tears for a few minutes. She pushed Honey back and took her cheeks in her warm hands. Honey was taller by several inches so she had to reach up. "Oh," the woman breathed, "you look like her a little, but you look like yourself a lot. Look at those eyes and that lovely, curly hair. Did your father have green eyes?"

"No."

Her grandma pulled her into another hug. "Your wolf is lovely too," she whispered into Honey's ear before she released her. "Come on, get in the car before they find us."

"You don't care that I'm part wolf or that knowing about me means you're cursed?"

"Well," her grandma said over the top of the car while she opened her door, "I would have preferred that your mother hadn't had to hide you, but I'm not afraid of a curse. I spent the last sixteen years wondering where my daughter was and why she'd never come home. No curse can be worse than that."

Honey slid into the car. It was both sad and terrible that her mom had gone into hiding when Honey was born and even worse that her grandmother would now never see her daughter again. Why had her mom not told her own mother what happened though? Had she done it simply to protect her mom from the curse or had she believed her mom would turn on her? Was climbing into the car mistake?

Her grandmother seemed nice, and Honey couldn't smell any duplicity around her, nor any charms. In fact, she smelled a little like her mom, like sunshine in the summer. They were both healers.

Her grandma's car was old and tan, but it was clean and cool inside.

"I'm so glad to meet you at last, Honey. Is Honey really your name?" Her grandma asked while she put the car in gear.

"That's all Mom ever called me."

"Tell me about your life, about where you grew up and went to school and everything. I've missed so much."

Honey didn't see how her grandma could use any of her past information against her, if she was so inclined, so she told her everything, even about her mom's business and how she used to help her make candles and soaps. She told her about her dad too and all the stuff they did when he visited. Her grandma nodded and listened, and occasionally wiped a tear from her eye. Honey considered suggesting they pull over, but there was hardly anyone on the roads and there were only a few tears. They headed east for a while, then turned onto a highway heading north. That's when she thought to ask where they were going.

"I'm taking you somewhere safe."

"No. I can't just disappear. I have friends. They'll be wondering what happened to me."

"It's better if you make a clean break."

"No it's not. They're wolves. I was basically adopted by the pack Luna and she never takes no for an answer. They'll keep searching for me until they find me. Also, I have a full scholarship. I just completed my first year of college. I want to finish."

Her grandma took her eyes off the road and looked at her in shock. "College! You're only fifteen."

Honey gave her a cheesy grin. "I skipped high school."

Her grandma turned back to the road with her brow furrowed. "Wait, you said you were home-schooled and that Maddie and you moved around a lot. How did you get into college?"

"Mom wanted me to go to high school so I could get used to being around other people. The school made me take the SAT to see what class I should be in. I got a perfect score. I could have applied for college then, but Mom wanted me to try high school first, so I went for one day."

"Just one?"

"Yeah."

"Why just one?"

She'd told the story enough times that she normally no longer cried when she repeated it, but after the horrible nightmares of the previous night she couldn't bring herself to tell it. "That's the day mom and dad died."

"How?" her grandma asked after several long seconds.

"Fire. The house burned down," Honey whispered.

"Did you see it? How did it catch fire?"

Should she tell her it was Gaian? Did her grandma like him? Was he like a son to her? Would it be too hard for her grandma to hear or would she even believe her?

Her grandma was around Gaian all the time as far as Honey could tell. She should know what he was capable of.

"Gaian told me he lost his temper."

"Gaian?"

"Yeah. He said he followed Mom from the store and found her and Dad together and confronted them in the house."

Grandma took a deep breath, then let out a long sigh. "Gaian. All those years waiting and then he does that. My poor little girl. I should have known he was involved when he started talking about moving on. He'd waited this long. Why the sudden change, I wondered, but did I listen to myself? No. I never really liked him, you know."

Tears were trickling down her round cheeks again.

"Maybe we should pull over. There's a fast-food place up ahead. I could eat."

"Oh, I should have thought of that. I bet you're hungry aren't you? When was the last time you ate?"

"Lunch, yesterday."

"You poor dear. You should have said something. What do you want? Hamburger? Fries?"

"I don't think they're serving that yet."

"Right. You're right. It's still breakfast time. So much has already happened this morning it seems later. Hashbrowns? Do you eat vegetables?"

Grandma didn't want to stay long in case someone had figured out Honey was with her, but she did let her go inside to use the restroom and wash her hands. In fact, she insisted Honey wash her hands. She probably thought they were filthy from running across the fields as a wolf. Honey didn't bother to tell her the dirt always disappeared when she transformed. Honey was positive her grandma had never been around any wolves before since she didn't ask how she'd transformed with her clothes on. Plus, she thought one breakfast sandwich would be enough. Honey talked her into three.

She could have escaped if she wanted to, but she was glad she finally got to meet her grandma and she didn't think her grandma meant her any harm.

"Where are we going?" Honey asked again when they were back on the road and she'd inhaled her first sandwich.

"London."

"London?" she choked.

"London, Canada."

"I can't go to Canada. I don't have a passport."

"Open the glove compartment."

Honey wiped the grease off her fingers and did as instructed. It was full of stuff, including dried herbs and seeds and a pack of cards.

"The yellow envelope."

Honey carefully worked the envelope out and looked inside. There was a piece of paper, several plastic cards, and a blue passport book. She reached in and pulled out the first card. "It's a driver's license."

"Mm-hm."

She inspected the picture. It looked a lot like her, but it wasn't quite her. "How did you know what I looked like?"

"It's a picture of your mom. Agnes said it would work."

"Agnes is your future-telling friend?"

"Seeing, and yes. You have a new name too. Isabelle Winters."

"Umm."

"I know. It's quite a change. I had a friend named Isabelle when I was little. I always liked that name. Winters is common enough among witches."

"But I'm not a witch."

"You're half-witch."

"Yes, but witches always detect my wolf side first."

"Feel around in the bottom of the envelope."

Honey did as she asked and pulled out a silver chain with a crescent-shaped pendant encircling a nearly transparent, round blue stone. "That's beautiful."

"It's yours. Happy birthday for the last fifteen years. Keep that safe. It was very hard to come by."

"Thanks."

"Put it on."

She caught a whiff of smoky fog when the stone slid past her nose. "It's a concealing charm?"

Her grandmother grinned. "Very good. Is that what your magic allows you to do, identify spells?"

"No. That's my wolf nose."

Her grandmother scrunched her own nose. "I didn't know wolves could identify spells with their noses."

"Most of them can only tell there's magic, not what it does. I was raised by a witch though."

Grandma made a non-committal noise and focused on the road. "As long as you wear that, no one should be able to detect you are a wolf, even other wolves, although we should test that before we get to our destination. I went ahead and got you a license even though you're only fifteen because we needed something to get into Canada and I thought it would be good to have in the event of an emergency. I do not want you driving without lessons though."

"I know how to drive. Mom and Dad started teaching me as soon as I could reach the pedals."

"Oh. Okay. Excellent. No driving though. You won't need a car where we are going."

"I won't?"

"Nope. I'm taking you to a boarding school for witches. It's in town so you can walk everywhere."

"But I'm a sophomore in college. I have a scholarship. I have friends. They're expecting me back. They're probably really worried about me."

"I know dear, but Agnes said it wouldn't be safe for me to take you back."

"And it's nearly summer," Honey pointed out. "School will be out soon if it isn't already, assuming they have the same schedule in Canada."

"You'll attend the last few weeks of the semester, then go to summer camp. An old friend of mine runs the school. I told her your parents died in an accident when you were little. I didn't say what kind. An aunt took you in, but she was nearly powerless, so she couldn't train you properly and she's gone now too. I didn't tell her we were related. I also told her I wasn't sure what kind of magic you have."

"Does this tell you?" Honey asked and pulled the CD-like object out of her pocket. She was still surprised it had fit.

Her grandmother glanced at it, then glanced again. "Yes. Where did you get that?"

"I found it on the table where Gaian had me tied up."

"Oh, that's," she shook her head. "Are you sure that's yours?"

Honey sniffed the blood in the center of the circle. "It doesn't smell like anyone else's. What does it mean?"

"The wedges that turn gold indicate your power. The more gold, the stronger your power. The power level on that is impressive if it's yours, considering you're only fifteen and you are only half-witch. The two powers are transmutation, probably due to your wolf, and," she glanced at the disk again. "abjuration which deals with protective spells and suppression of other's magic. Does that make sense to you? Can you cast protective spells?"

"Kind of? I've only tried a few times."

"You broke through the wards, didn't you? I was concerned you wouldn't be able to escape, but Agnes told me you'd figure it out."

"Yeah. I just had to pull the strands apart."

"What do you mean?"

"If I focus, I can see the spells and sometimes manipulate them."

"Definitely abjuration then." She was quiet for a few moments then said, "This is good. I can tell her I tested you and just mention abjuration. That way she won't find out that you have a second specialty."

Her grandma drove north until they hit Chicago, then took 94 East. She'd left her phone at home because she didn't want anyone to track them, so they used a map. Grandma was impressed Honey knew how to read one, but her mom had never used a phone to navigate places either. They stopped for a few minutes to take a look at Lake Michigan, then headed for Detroit.

Honey talked her grandmother into stopping for more food in Ann Arbor, which was about twenty miles outside of Detroit. Grandma put on a big floppy hat and did the ordering while Honey wore a black baseball hat with 'USA' on the front and went to the restroom. Three teenage girls were crammed together in front of the mirror inside the restroom making fishy faces at one of the girls' phones. Perfect.

Honey pointed to the phone. "Hey, can I borrow that?"

"For what?"

She huffed out a sigh. "I lost my phone. I need to text my guardian so he doesn't call in the army." She had decided not to say dad in case the girl was questioned.

"Oh, sure."

"Thanks."

Watching miles of green pass by had given her plenty of time to think of a message. She typed in bio-dad's real number and sent, *"Borrowed phone. I'm OK. With friend. It was mom's ex, both times. I'll send you a postcard.-H"* She wouldn't, but hopefully he'd figure out it meant she'd be gone for a while.

She handed the phone back to the girl with an honest smile and a thanks, then did what she'd come in to do. The girls were gone when she finished. She stepped out of the bathroom and was nearly plowed over by a group of young man, wolves who'd been out for a run by the musk emanating from them.

"Watch it, witch."

40

"What?" She should smell like a human to him if the charm was working. Did she do some magic without realizing it?

"Are you threatening me?"

"No." Where had he gotten that idea?

Her curled the corner of his lip like he was smelling something unpleasant. "Lies stink, you know."

"Okay."

He sniffed at her and curled his nose even more. "You smell like a lie."

Uh oh.

"Weird."

She slipped past him, between his friends, and then out the door, leaving her grandma behind as they had planned. Maybe that's why her mom had never got her a concealment charm. Hiding her wolf side from witches would have made their lives so much easier, but not if it made wolves suspicious.

She unlocked the door and slid into the passenger seat, then cranked back the seat so it would be harder for people to see her. Surely bio-dad would let her friends know she was okay. They had probably freaked out when she didn't show up for their after-finals party. How had Gaian found her? Had he told anyone what she was? Would she be able to go back to school next year?

Unless Gaian vanished or conveniently forgot about her, she didn't see how she could. Wait, she had abjuration powers – protection powers. Could her powers be used to make a bad person forget things? Or maybe she could she use them to fix the charm so she could blend in among witches without worrying about suspicious wolves whenever she wanted. Too bad the librarian at college already knew she was a wolf. Hold on. The witch school probably had a library. She could read up on curses over the summer and find a way to help Zavier break that curse on the land! This was good.

4

WITCH SCHOOL

"Isabelle, this is Wanda, a long-time friend of mine." Honey's grandmother gestured toward the tallish, sturdily built woman with salt-and-pepper hair who had stood to greet them when they walked into her office.

The woman grabbed Honey's offered hand in both of hers and gave it a single, firm shake. "That's Ms. Charming to you, but welcome, Isabelle."

"Thank you."

Ms. Charming gestured toward two wooden chairs with red vinyl seats and arms that were aligned perfectly with the large desk in front of them. "Have a seat."

Honey sat while still taking in the décor. Dark wood shelves backed with white lined two adjacent walls from floor to ceiling. Red and/or shiny items were interspersed with clusters of books. A series whose bindings fit together to form a long blue wave against an orange background snagged her attention. The gold titles had names like 'Conjuration for the Creative' and 'Divination at a Distance'.

"You have a good eye, Isabelle," Ms. Charming commented.

Honey tore her eyes off the books and focused on the woman. "Sorry."

"No, no. From what Mrs. Wixx tells me, you haven't had a chance to read many magical texts. It's good that you are curious. Those particular books are part of a series written by witches who are experts in their fields. I was asked to write a few chapters in 'Enchantment for the Charming' myself. It's coming out in the fall. What have you read?"

Telling her about all the books she'd read on curses was undoubtedly not the way to go. "Very little. My m..aunt didn't have many books."

Completely true. She and mom had moved a lot. Books were heavy, and it would be weird for 'humans' to have magical books, not that they ever invited anyone into the house.

"Ah, that's too bad. I don't think kids read enough today. What kind of training have you had?"

"As I said, very little," Honey's grandmother interrupted. "She's been tested though. Her talents lean toward abjuration."

"Hmm. That a good one. You can earn a steady income making protective charms even if you don't have a lot of magic. Was your mother also gifted with abjuration?"

"No," Honey answered before her grandmother could. "Healing."

"What about your dad?"

"Transmutation."

Dad would have laughed if he heard that.

Ms. Charming nodded. "That's odd, but not unheard of. You probably inherited it from an ancestor."

Honey had no idea if she had, so she just looked at the woman.

Ms. Charming opened a folder on her desk. "I'll need your school records eventually, but I can put you in the same classes you were in back home. What grade are you, 10, 11?"

"She was home schooled," her grandmother said quickly.

"I'm taking college classes," Honey added. "I just finished my freshman year."

"I thought you were sixteen?"

"She skipped a few grades," her grandmother said. "But she's woefully behind in her magic."

"If you give me the lesson plans for the freshman class, I'll see if I can catch up," Honey volunteered.

The woman dismissed Honey's idea with a shake of her head. "It's not just reading, it's experimentation too and you'll need an experienced witch to supervise."

"Why don't you let her assist in the magic classes for the next few weeks," her grandmother suggested. "She might be able to pick something up, then the magic teachers will be better able to suggest where she should be placed for summer classes."

"I'm not sure she'll be able to assist much if she doesn't know magic."

"I know some things, mostly about healing, and I'm a very quick learner."

"Hmm, I'll introduce you to Miss Evelstone, our newest magic teacher. She can use some assistance. I'll also

45

find you some texts on abjuration so you can begin exploring your talent."

"Thank you."

The woman opened a notebook and jotted something in the middle of a page. "I'm going to put you in with a few of the older girls until the end of the semester. We can shuffle you around to something more appropriate once the semester is over. Jessica is one of my top students. Her power is illusion, but she will be able to help you with basic magic concepts."

"Thank you."

"If you get your things, I'll have someone take you up there now."

"Sure."

"I wasn't sure if she needed bedding or a pillow," Grandma said.

Ms. Charming dismissed her concern with a wave. "That's taken care of in the fee, unless she needs something special."

"No," Honey said.

"Good. One of the girls will meet you at the door to show you to your room. Unfortunately, you missed dinner."

"She just ate," her grandma said.

"Shocking how much teenage girls can put away, isn't it?" Ms. Charming said knowingly. "Would you care for some tea, Rachel? I thought we could catch up."

"I'm afraid I still need to find a room for the night."

"I have a guest room. You can stay here."

"I don't want to cause any trouble."

"It's no trouble Rachel. It really isn't." She wiggled her fingers, "The sheets in the guest room are charmed to be self-cleaning."

Grandma laughed. It was the first time Honey had seen her truly smile. "Remember the first time you tried that charm?"

Her friend laughed with her. "How could I forget?"

"Her brother's friend couldn't stay on the bed. He kept slipping off. Real dirt-bag, that one," her grandma chuckled.

Grandma tossed Honey a key. "Here Hon…." Her grandma's mouth was poised to say the 'ey' but she caught herself in time. "Go get your things. Bring me back the key."

"Okay."

She hadn't seen the school in the light, since it was dark when they arrived, but even in the dark, the big old Victorian house/school was pretty. It even had a tower. She opened the back door and retrieved the duffel bag already filled with the clothes she and Grandma had bought after they'd arrived in town. They'd been lucky to find a thrift store with so many shirts in Honey's size. Canadian prices were higher than American, but they still managed to find enough clothes to fill the bag for the equivalent of less than a hundred American dollars including a couple of hoodies and a coat. New underwear and toiletries had put them over, but not by much. Her grandma still had enough cash to get home so no one would know she'd spent time and money in Canada.

A slim girl, just a hair shorter than Honey, was waiting at the door. Her brown hair was perfectly smooth, her pale skin flawless, and her shirt and pants wrinkle-free. The girl raised a manicured eyebrow and scanned Honey's less-than-pristine T-shirt and jeans with a less-than-happy look. Honey stuck out her hand.

"Hi, I'm Isabelle Winters."

Honey could smell her own lie. How could witches not?

The girl looked down at Honey's hand and didn't curl her lip, but she might as well have. It was going to be like that then. Honey retracted her hand and used it to adjust the duffel bag.

"Jessica," the girl said and turned her back on Honey. "This way."

Jessica led her back through the open, wood-lined foyer to a beautiful set of stairs with smooth wooden rails supported by ornate spindles. A long hall extended from the landing on the second floor toward the back of the house. It looked longer than she would have guessed it could be, but she hadn't seen the back of the house from the street. Jessica led her about halfway down the hall, then stopped in front of a red-stained wooden door with a pale green vine painted around the outside.

She shot Honey a look over her shoulder. "The door is spelled so only the people who belong here can get in."

"Okay."

"You will have to wait for one of us to let you in."

"Us who?"

"Myself and my roommates, Wyn and Trix."

"Okay."

"You won't like what happens if you try to enter without us."

"What will happen?"

Jessica stepped back and waved at the door. "Try and see."

"That's okay. I'm good." She'd sniff it out later when Jessica wasn't watching.

Jessica shrugged with her eyebrows and turned the knob.

Inside looked nothing like Honey's college dorm or her friends' suite. The room was big, bigger than it should be based on the proximity to the next door down the hall. It was shaped like a clover with the door where the stem would be. Each leaf had a full-size bed and abounded with feminine decorations. The one to Honey's left had vines and fairy lights. The one to her right was predominantly pink and fluffy while the one in front was blue and gray and sleek.

"Wow," she said appreciatively.

Jessica gestured disdainfully at an uncomfortable looking cot behind the comfy-looking couch right in front of them. "That's for you."

"Looks comfy."

"I didn't mean the couch."

"I know."

It was all an illusion. Over the scents of the three girls, Honey could smell smoke with a touch of deceit. She could also smell a floral scent that tingled with a touch of camphor and the faint smell of a dead mouse. The mouse smell was coming from the pink room. She really hoped something hadn't died in all that fluff.

"What are you doing?" Jessica asked.

Honey realized she'd been sniffing in the direction of the pink room. Oops. She had to remember the witches here thought she was a witch.

"Thought I smelled something."

"Probably Wyn's candles. She has a collection."

"Ah."

Jessica gestured toward a cardboard box in a corner that was remarkably dusty and neglected considering the rest of the room. "You can store your stuff there."

"Actually, I need to do some laundry. Where do I go for that?"

"Basement. Come on, I'll show you."

The corner of Jessica's mouth wiggled a little when she turned toward the door. That didn't bode well. The girl was up to something, but whatever it was, was probably better than staying in this room.

After giving the key back to her grandma, who was drinking something stronger than tea out of a delicate teacup if Honey's nose was correct, she followed Jessica into the back of the house on the ground floor. Again, the back of the school extended farther than she expected, but they didn't go into the hall. Jessica led her through the first door into a kitchen and then immediately to a smaller door, which she opened.

"Here." She reached in and pulled a string hanging from a bare bulb.

A set of dusty, cobweb-lined wooden steps led down into what smelled like an old cellar. It didn't smell like an illusion, nor did it smell like there was a washing machine anywhere near.

"You'll need to show me how to use the washer. Why don't you go first."

"You don't know how to use a washer?" the girl scoffed.

"I know how to use a washer, but they're all different. Go ahead. I'll follow you."

To her surprise, Jessica started down the stairs. At the bottom of the stairs, she turned to the right to walk around a large stone pillar that might have once been a fireplace, then turned right again towards the back of the room. There was nothing there but a brick wall. Jessica looked back over her shoulder with a smirk and tapped one of the bricks with her index finger. The whole wall vanished.

The low-ceilinged, dark basement abruptly expanded into a long, well-lit room with white walls, dark floors, and a row of colorful couches placed back-to-back down the middle. A big piece of glass formed a window in the closest wall through which she could see a row of washers. Further along the walls were more doors, all with windows in the walls next to them. The room again extended farther than Honey expected towards the back of the building.

"Classrooms," Jessica explained.

"There are classrooms in the basement?"

"Most magic classes are down here. It's safer. Come on. I'll explain the washers."

She actually did, to Honey's amazement. Maybe Jessica wasn't so bad.

"Thank you. Look, I know you don't want me in your room with your friends and I don't want to intrude. Ms. Charming said it was only temporary."

"Why are you here?"

"To go to school."

"Why? What did you do to get kicked out of your old one?"

"I wasn't. My," she started to mention her parents, but that might be a clue to someone. "It's a long, convoluted story."

"Ms. C said your parents are dead."

"Yes," Honey agreed with a sigh.

"You're an orphan."

Ouch. "I can't help what I am any more than you can help who you are."

"That's where you're wrong." Jessica changed before her eyes into a tall, curvy model with red lips and blond hair, filling the air around her with a smoky candle smell.

"I think you're prettier the other way," Honey said truthfully, "and what you look like on the outside doesn't change who you are on the inside."

Jessica's form morphed into the original one, complete with curled lip. "You sound like my mother."

"Does she have illusion magic too?"

"Yes."

"Then she would know."

Jessica gave a disbelieving grunt and nodded toward a cabinet. "The detergent is in there. My friends and I will probably be in the room when you're done. Just knock." She stepped to the door and looked back with what

Honey could only describe as a feral grin. "Oh and watch out for the rats. They bite."

It wasn't rats. It was snakes when Honey opened the cabinet, but she had smelled Jessica cast her spell before she left the room, so she knew something would be there. The snakes looked and sounded real but her nose and the knowledge that king cobras did not live in Canada made her pretty confident they were illusions. Curious, she studied them with her magical sight. If she hadn't seen them with her normal sight, she wouldn't even know they were there. It was only when she looked between the molecules, that she saw the shapes. Interesting. She swiped her hand through one. The stuff in-between scattered, then coalesced back into a snake shape. She reached between them to grab some detergent. One of the snakes lunged at her and bit her hand. It looked like the teeth were buried so deep they should be going through the other side, but she didn't feel a thing. The molecules in her hand and the spaces between them were unperturbed.

Someone screamed.

A short girl with generous curves and wavy, light brown hair, stood in the doorway behind Honey. She was probably pretty, but all Honey noticed was her open mouth and the piercing sound shooting out of it. Honey shook her hand and the illusion flew across the room to disappear when it hit the wall. Why did it do that? Did the spell just happen to cease at the same moment it hit the wall or did hitting the wall disrupt it so much it ceased?

"Oh my gosh, are you okay?" the girl asked.

Honey looked down at her hand and refocused her sight. As she suspected, no fang marks. "I'm fine. It was only an illusion."

"Are you sure? It looked so real."

"Yeah."

All the snakes in the cabinet were gone too. Honey walked to the first washer to put the detergent in.

"Wait, did you hear me?"

"Yes." She glanced back at the door. No one was there. She switched back to her magic sight and the girl came into focus.

"Can you see me?" the girl asked.

"Yes."

The girl clasped her hands together and let out a huge sigh. "Oh, thank God! I thought I was going to have to live like that the rest of my life."

"Like what?"

"Invisible. Silent. Gone."

"Oh."

"Don't use that washer," the girl said, coming to stand beside her. "It eats clothes."

Honey looked inside the washer she'd just opened. "Really?"

"Yeah, and the second one makes them dirtier, but the third one usually works."

"What about the fourth one?"

"I don't know. I haven't seen anyone try."

"How long have you been here?" Honey asked her.

"I started last fall," the girl said. "I haven't seen you before. Are you new?"

"Yeah." Honey scanned the molecules of the first washer and then the between. It was definitely spelled, as were the second and the third, but the fourth looked all right. She dropped her duffel bag in front of it and poured in some detergent.

"I'm Frederica," the girl said.

"H.." Honey coughed and cleared her throat, then sent the girl a smile over her shoulder. "Sorry. My name is Isabelle."

The clothes reeked of thrift store and new clothes. Honey wondered if the girl could tell. She'd taken all the labels off and opened the new packages of underwear in the car in case someone watched her unpack, but she couldn't fix the smell. To hurry things along, she took the little bag with her new toiletries out of the duffel bag, then dumped everything else inside the washer including the duffel bag. To further cover the smell, she poured more detergent over the top.

"Have you ever done laundry before?" the girl asked.

"Yep." Honey turned a knob and pushed a button. It started, so Jessica must not have lied about that part.

"That's a lot of detergent."

Honey turned her back on the washer and gave her mysterious new friend a grin. "I like my clothes to smell clean. Were you going to wash something too?"

"Oh, no. I was just…" she waved toward the door.

"What?" Honey urged when the girl didn't continue.

"Watching you. I have never seen you around and I'm stuck down here."

"What do you mean?"

"Yesterday Victoria told me to shut up and disappear and since then I haven't been able to leave this floor."

"Who's Victoria?" Honey asked.

"My sister."

"And no one has looked for you?"

The girl shrugged.

Honey switched to her normal sight and then back again. The girl looked whole and her molecules acted like they were part of a solid human, but she disappeared under normal light.

"Why are you looking at me like that?" Frederica asked.

"You look solid, but you keep disappearing."

"I'm not a ghost, if that's what you're thinking."

"I wasn't." Honey focused on the edge of Frederica's shape. Now she could see it. The space in-between the molecules around Frederica formed a thin, transparent layer of brown. It smelled like a dusty cloak that had been hanging in the attic for years and looked almost solid enough to grab. She reached up and wrapped her fingers around the transparent lining by Frederica's head. It acted just like the thin blanket she envisioned. With a quick jerk, she pulled it off and let it fall on the floor where it vanished the moment it made contact. Honey flipped back to her normal sight. She'd broke the spell! Frederica was visible.

Frederica looked at her shoulder and then back at Honey. "What did you do?"

"Oh, I thought I saw a hair or something. Your sister must have spelled you on accident. Looks like it's wearing off."

Frederica snorted. "It was no accident, or maybe it was. She's not really good at spells." She stretched out her hand and knocked on the door. "Can you hear that?"

"Yeah."

Frederica gave a sigh of relief. "No matter how much noise I made no one could hear me and when I tried to pick up a pen to leave a message I couldn't pick it up. It was awful. You hungry? I've been stuck down here since yesterday. I've only eaten a couple of cookies and a fruit bar that someone had in their backpack."

"I could eat."

"Come on then. Let's go to the kitchen, then I'll give you a tour if you want."

"Sure."

5

NOT A GHOST

Frederica used a password, *aperta*, to get out of the basement. No wonder Jessica had been so eager to take Honey to the basement. She would have never thought to say 'open' in Latin and wave her hand at the door.

Frederica talked non-stop even while stuffing herself with two cheese and peanut-butter sandwiches. Honey listened and nodded appropriately and sipped the hot chocolate Frederica had insisted she try. Afterward, Frederica gave Honey a tour of the school. Empty offices and classrooms for human classes like French and math were on the first floor. The second floor, where Honey had already been, was also empty, as was the third floor where the students in Grades 9 and 10 (not freshmen and sophomore, Honey noted) were housed.

"Where is everyone?"

"Oh, it's Friday. A lot of people go home on Friday or they might be watching a movie in the lounge. Every other Friday is movie night."

"Really?"

Frederica scrunched her nose. "Don't get too excited. They're usually old and boring. Come on, I'll show you the library."

The library was hidden in the tower in plain sight. To human visitors, it would look like an old-fashioned sitting room with ancient books all around, which was exactly what it was, except the titles were obscured and the books were spelled to repel humans so they never tried to read them. It was much smaller than the college library at Vindale U. Honey took a quick look around. She didn't see anything on molecular chemistry, or any science, but she did find some history books.

"Can I check these out?" she asked pulling out the oldest one.

"Sure," Frederica said. "You just tell the big book you're going to borrow it and it will put down your name."

"The big book?"

"Yeah." Frederica pointed toward a large, white book at least three feet wide open on a stand near an ornate fireplace.

Nearing it, Honey could make out a long list of handwritten titles and names that filled half of the first page. Some had been crossed out.

She held up the history book. "Um, Big Book, I'd like to check this book out."

Nothing happened.

"No, like this," Frederica said. She stepped up with a small paperback. "Grand Livre, Frederica Felix, checking out 'The Curious Cat'."

Letters formed in the book like someone was writing them with an old-fashioned feather pen, but there wasn't one there.

"Wow."

"I know. Cool, right? To return the book you say the same thing except 'returning' instead of checking out. Now you try."

"Grand Livre, Isabelle Winters checking out 'The History of Witches, Volume I'."

Nothing happened.

"I've never seen it not work before," Frederica commented beside her.

"Maybe it's because I'm new. Maybe the book knows who's enrolled and my name hasn't been added yet," Honey hedged, but she suspected it was because the book knew Isabelle wasn't her real name.

"Maybe, or that's considered a reference book and can't be checked out, or it could be your accent. You're from the States, aren't you? Try one of the reading books."

Honey hadn't read for pleasure in ages, but she didn't want to try and have that fail in front of Frederica too. "We can come back later. I better go check my laundry. It's probably done if the washer hasn't eaten it."

"Oh, right, I forgot about that. I'll go with you. You have to be careful which dryer you use too."

"Thank you. You sure you don't want to watch the movie?"

"I'm sure."

Her clothes were fine. Two of the four driers were also spelled. She wanted to try and break the spells but not with Frederica there. She knew she was supposed to be a witch now, but it felt weird to do magic in front of other witches.

"What is your magical specialty," Honey asked, once the drier had started successfully.

"Portals," Frederica said proudly, "like my dad. My power level tested pretty high but my powers haven't manifested yet. Once they do though, I'll be able to join my dad and grandfather. Portal makers are in high demand because we're rare and it takes several to make a stable portal. A single portal maker can make a portal, but they usually only last a minute or so."

"Cool."

"What about you?"

"Abjuration."

"What branch?"

"Um…"

"It's probably whatever your mom or dad could do."

"It's not."

"Oh. Well, it's a useful power to have, no matter what your specialty is. Some people have even found a way to make money by banishing things."

"Banishing things?"

"Yeah. Have a bunch of junk in your yard? They can banish it."

"Banish it to where?"

Frederica shrugged.

Is that what happened to her clothes when she transformed? Honey made a mental note to look it up later when her new friend wasn't watching over her shoulder. She had mostly full access to a magical library!

There was something else she wanted to do first that Frederica would undoubtedly be glad to help her with.

"Can you give me a tour of the classrooms down here? I've never taken a classroom class on magic."

"Oh, sure!"

6

GOODBYE

It was getting late.

Honey talked Frederica into showing her where her room was on the third floor, then left with her soapy-smelling duffel bag full of freshly laundered and folded clothes presumably to go to her assigned room where her new roommates were undoubtedly congratulating Jessica on locking her in the basement. After the day and night she'd had, she didn't feel like dealing with them, so after taking a shower and brushing her teeth in the communal bathroom on the third floor, Honey went back to the library. It was a little chilly, but she had warm clothes and there was a vintage camelback couch that didn't look too uncomfortable.

After a thorough search of the library shelves, she settled again on the history book. Several failed attempts to get past the first sentence later, she leaned her head back on the back of the sofa to stare at the center point at the top of the tower. What had Liam and Walter and Luca and Nathan done when she hadn't shown up last night? Had Brayton gone alpha on them when she disappeared? Surely Alpha Silver passed her message on to Luna Lynn and Lynn would have told her friends so they'd know she was okay.

Her heart hurt thinking of all the things she and her friends had been planning to do together over the summer. She sniffed and wiped her cheeks with the sleeve of her new/old hoodie. She did need to learn how to use her magic, and how to break Zavier's curse and perhaps her own, if it existed. This was the perfect opportunity, but still, she already missed her friends. She should have memorized their numbers instead of relying on her phone to keep track of them all the time.

Giving up on the book, she set it carefully on the floor and laid her head on her duffel bag. What she really wished was that she could sleep once again in her bed under the quilt her mom had made with her mom just down the hall, or better, with her mom beside her. She arranged one of the hoodies over her legs and the coat over her torso. At least she wouldn't have to worry about anyone smelling or hearing her tears when she cried.

Hours later, she woke to a stuffy nose, a headache, and a beam of morning sun dancing over a room full of unread magic books. If she had to be apart from her friends, this was a great place to be. She sat up and stretched, knocking the hoodie and the coat to the floor. Despite its thin cushions, the couch had been a decent bed. Would anyone notice if she slept in here for the next two weeks? She scooped up the hoodie and the coat and stuffed them back into the bag. If she could find a good place to stash her stuff, it might be doable, and it would prevent the mean girls from messing with it.

Unfortunately, the room was hexagonal in shape and all the furniture was in the middle. The only space to stash anything was under the couch but it had thin wooden legs and no fabric of any sort hanging down that could disguise her bag. She wound up leaving the bag in the shadow of the fireplace mantel behind the big book until she could find somewhere better. After putting the history book back on the shelf and finger-combing her hair into a messy knot, she stepped out into the entryway on the first floor.

"Honey! There you are. We've been looking all over for you."

Her grandmother hurried across the room in sight of several students and Ms. Charming. Did she realize she'd just blown her cover? "Oh sorry, Mrs. Wixx. I was in the library."

"The one place we didn't look," her grandmother huffed over her shoulder to the matron. She turned back to Honey and took her hand. "Isabelle, I have to leave you now. You think you'll be all right here?"

"I'll be fine."

Grandma let go of her hand with a little sigh and looked resolutely toward the door. A handshake just wasn't appropriate to say goodbye to the mother of her mother. Honey pulled her into a hug.

"Thank you, Mrs. Wixx, for bringing me here. I really appreciate it."

Her grandmother hugged her back. Honey clung to her longer than she would have if she was truly a stranger but released her in plenty of time so that it wasn't odd. "You be careful on the road. Pull over if you get tired," Honey admonished.

Her grandmother rolled her eyes. "What are you, my mother?"

"Ha, ha."

Grandma dug into her purse and pulled out an envelope. "Here. I wrote my number on this. You call me if you need anything."

The envelope wasn't empty. Honey quickly stuffed it into her pocket. "Okay."

They stood in the entry for a few seconds awkwardly starting at each other. Grandma looked like she was about to tear up.

"Shall I carry your bag out to the car?" Honey thought to say, indicating the extra-large purse which doubled as an overnight bag on her grandma's shoulder.

"I can handle it," Grandma said loud enough for anyone near to hear, then more quietly. "I need to handle it."

"Okay."

Her grandmother looked at the door and released a deep sigh.

"Rachel, is something wrong?" Ms. Charming asked.

"No, just not looking forward to that drive."

"Better get started."

"I know."

Her grandma patted Honey on the arm. "You take care."

"Come on," Ms. Charming said, putting her arm through her grandma's, "I'll walk you out."

And that was the last Honey saw of her grandma for a long time.

7

DANGEROUS DOORKNOB

"Isabelle! Isabelle!"

Honey turned around to see who the person was shouting at and realized it was herself.

"Good Morning, Frederica."

Frederica's nearly flawless skin was no longer flawless. Inflamed, painful-looking pimples covered her whole face.

"What happened?" spilled out of Honey's mouth before she realized how rude it might be.

Frederica gingerly reached for her face but didn't touch it. "I went to your room and knocked on the door. When no one answered, I touched the doorknob." She said it nonchalantly, but her eyes were shiny with tears. "They told me you never showed up last night. I thought maybe I'd just imagined you."

Honey felt her hands start to change. She quickly clenched her fists so Frederica wouldn't notice her nails lengthening. What was wrong with her? She'd never accidentally transformed when she got made before. Maybe living with wolves the last two semesters had rubbed off on her.

"They cursed the doorknob to do that? That's awful. Is there a healer here?"

"Yeah."

"Let's go see her."

"She's probably still sleeping."

"We'll wake her up then. She wouldn't want you to suffer because she's sleeping."

Frederica led her to the administrative side of the first floor near Ms. Charming's office. A plump woman in her late thirties or early forties answered the door, took one look at Frederica, and dragged her inside, tsking with her tongue.

The woman plopped Frederica down on an examination table and started pulling bottles and jars from a shelf. Honey read the labels while the healer pinched and squeezed and poured the different ingredients together. The healer's concoction was similar to the blemish cream her own mother had used to make, but more concentrated and with a few extra ingredients. To finish, the healer stirred the mixture exactly three times with a small wooden spoon, tapped it once on the side of the little pot, then handed the pot to Frederica.

"Here, smear all of this on your face. There's a little mirror there. Make sure you get every bit of your skin covered or the spell will pop up where you missed. It has to set for thirty minutes after you're covered."

Frederica nodded and dutifully took the pot.

The healer turned on Honey. "I haven't seen you before. Tell me what happened."

"She touched the doorknob to Jessica's room."

The healer sighed and shook her head. "That spell. Most of the injuries I treat are due to the girls spelling one another either on accident or on purpose, but that spell is one of the worst. Thank goodness the one who can cast it is graduating this year."

"Does the spell disappear once someone touches it?"

"No, unfortunately, but it will fade over time."

"Is it legal to spell the doorknob?"

"It's not against the rules as long as no permanent harm is done. The girls are allowed to protect their rooms and belongings however they see fit. It encourages learning and caution."

Honey glanced at Frederica who was still diligently smearing green goop on her pus-laden cheeks. "A painful lesson."

"Indeed. What's your name?"

Her mouth formed an 'H' but she caught herself just in time. "Isabelle Winters."

"By your lack of knowledge of the rules, I gather you are new. You've come very late in the semester though."

"I already finished my semester back home. I was taking college classes. I came here to learn magic."

"College classes?" Frederica squeaked. "How old are you?"

"Don't talk," the nurse admonished. "Smear. You have to get it on quickly, before it stops working."

"I skipped a few grades," Honey informed Frederica, "but I didn't have the opportunity to take classes on magic."

"What branch of magic will you be studying," the nurse asked.

"Abjuration, but I used to help a healer prepare her potions. I recognized most of the ingredients you used, but what is this?" She pointed to a little bottle of powder labeled 'ground Opuntia spines'.

"Those are ground thorns from a prickly pear cactus. It's useful for counteracting spells. Very potent. You only need a pinch, generally."

"Is this supposed to sting?" Frederica asked.

"It might," the nurse replied. "It shouldn't last long though."

"Okay." Frederica's voice wobbled and a tear escaped the corner of her eye.

It wasn't fair. Frederica shouldn't have been punished just for touching a doorknob. Stupid bullies. They were probably having a good laugh.

"Will you be all right here for a little while?"

"She will be fine," the nurse said. "She's going to lay back and close her eyes and rest while the salve does its work. She needs to keep her face still."

Honey patted Frederica's arm. "I'll be back."

"Where are you going?"

"To keep anyone else from getting hurt, hopefully."

"What are you going to do?"

"I don't know yet. Maybe put up a sign?" She gave the girl an encouraging pat and a smile and exited the room. She wasn't sure what she was going to do, but it would be better than a sign.

There were a lot more girls roaming the halls than there had been the night before. Most of them were near the kitchen and the dining room. They didn't pay any attention to Honey. She kept her focus forward and walked purposely past them and up the stairs. The few girls walking down the second-floor hallway gave her a brief glance, then ignored her as well.

With her magical sight, the spell on the door was obvious. It looked like a dark red ribbon flowing around the knob until she reached for it with her hand, then the red flowed into the space above the knob and formed an angry-looking face with a mouth full of teeth that reminded her strongly of Brayton's wolf. It followed the movement of the finger she waved in the air over its head with barred teeth. It even had specks of saliva running from the corners of its mouth. Apparently, she wouldn't be able to simply pull off the spell like she had the one on Frederica.

"What are you doing?"

Honey jumped and jerked her hand away. Three girls stood at her back. By the smells, the blond and the dark-haired girls behind Jessica were Trix and Wyn, Honey's other two roommates.

"Why do you have such a nasty spell on the doorknob?" Honey asked.

"To keep out losers."

She thought of saying 'too bad it didn't work' but that would make her as bad as they were, so she didn't say anything.

"Are you going to stand in our way all day?" Jessica asked after they'd stared at each other for several seconds.

"Oh, sorry."

Honey stepped back to stand against the wall next to do the door. She switched to her other sight again when Jessica reached for the knob. The girl paused just before she touched it, long enough for the spell to sniff at her hand. The wolf scrunched its nose, then flowed away from the knob and onto the door like water.

"What are you looking at?" Jessica demanded.

"Your hand. You have a lovely hand."

Jessica frowned at Honey like she'd stepped in a cow patty. "You're weird."

Honey grinned. Better they think she was harmless than know the truth. "Believe it or not, you aren't the first to say that."

Jessica rolled her eyes and shook her head while she turned the knob. "Ugh. How to do we always get stuck with the losers."

"You must have bad luck. I usually get stuck with the nice people," Honey said as seriously as she could.

Jessica stepped into the room, probably still rolling her eyes. Wyn followed right behind her. Trix paused. She was what the guys would have called cute with her heart-shaped face and wavy blond hair pulled back into a messy bun. She even had freckles. She nodded at the doorknob.

"Go ahead. You know you want to."

The scents of camphor and fragrant flowers flowed around her. She knew Trix was spelling her, but it didn't stop her from raising her hand. Curious, she watched while her arm was covered in a thin pink veil that kind of floated it toward the knob. Interestingly, Trix's spell was not only making her move, it was soothing too. Oh! Maybe that's how she could tame the spell.

"That's it. You're almost there," Trix encouraged.

The spell barred its teeth. Honey urged the pink to flow off her arm and around the beast guarding the doorknob. Its lips quivered, then she swore she heard it whimper.

"You poor thing. It's no fun guarding a door all day, is it," she cooed under her breath. The spell ducked its head. Something told her it was not tamed, just momentarily confused. She touched it anyway, running one finger over the top of its little head. It looked like it was trying to growl and whimper at the same time. "There. Does that feel good? You like that don't you."

The spell's head drooped, then bounced, then suddenly disappeared altogether.

"Huh."

"You realize you are petting the doorknob?" Jessica asked with one eyebrow raised.

"Am I?" It probably did look like that to them.

Had she disabled the spell permanently or just calmed it for now like Jessica had? She'd check it out later when the three mean girls weren't watching over her shoulder.

"Why isn't she breaking out?" the dark-haired girl who smelled faintly of dead mouse asked.

Honey guessed she was the necromancer. Was she also the one who'd made the spell? Honey knew necromancers used life forces and could cast spells, which might explain why the spell had acted like an animal, but if the girl had cast it, wouldn't she be able to tell the spell had accepted her?

"Maybe it needs a recharge," Trix said. "It sounded like it zapped whoever that was pretty good earlier."

"I believe it was a friend of yours," Jessica smirked at Honey. "Stupid 9th years. You think they would have learned by now."

Honey refused to give the bully the pleasure of her attention. Instead, since she was basically in the room now since she'd stepped inside to reach the knob on the open door, she looked past Jessica and Wyn and studied the illusion. The blue/gray room was not at the top of a clover, but at the top left of the large square which contained four rooms. The fourth room was beyond the couch and undecorated. The cot behind the couch was actually a box that would have probably collapsed if she'd tried to lay on it. It looked like a nice room. Too bad the neighborhood was so unfriendly.

"What are you looking at?" Jessica demanded.

"The wall, clearly." She could have walked through the illusion and claimed the room, but there was no point. She wouldn't feel comfortable sleeping with those three around.

"Did you get your laundry done?" Jessica asked with a smirk.

"I did, thank you," Honey smiled politely.

"Why didn't you come to bed then?" Jessica asked knowingly.

"I didn't want to disturb you," Honey blinked innocently. "I know how important sleep is, especially for children."

"Are you calling us children?"

"Actions speak louder than words." Not the best put-down she could have come up with. Oh well. "You can put the room back to the way it was. I found somewhere I like better."

"Good," Jessica snapped.

"Yeah, good," the blond echoed.

"What do you mean, back the way it was," the necromancer asked suspiciously.

Honey flashed a toothy grin, then walked away. There were a few witches at college who had bad attitudes, but none as bad as the girls she'd just left. Was nastiness a common trait of high school witches or was it just ones in boarding school? She wished she could ask her witch roommate from college.

8

YOU SHOULD BE DRY

She spent Saturday exploring London with Frederica in tow. It was a nice town with a convenient layout. A shopping center and a library were just blocks away, and a few blocks beyond them was the Thames River with a paved running trail that went for miles. A few blocks the other way was a martial arts academy. She didn't have any money except the two-hundred Canadian dollars her grandmother had left her in cash, but maybe they would let her teach in exchange for mat time. To top it all off, there was a university only a few kilometers north that she could get to by bus, according to the pamphlet she picked up from the public library. She just had to figure out how to pay for classes in the event she had to stay.

Sunday morning, Honey opened her eyes to Frederica watching her from a nearby chair. Honey had told Frederica where she was sleeping to explain why she wanted to buy a blanket at the thrift store, but having the girl staring at her when she woke up was too much. Frederica didn't even seem to realize it was weird.

"Good morning, Isabelle!"

Honey held back her groan and forced out a small smile instead. "Good morning, Frederica."

The girl grinned like Honey had given her a present. Most of Honey's annoyance dissipated immediately.

"What do you want to do today? It's raining but we could go back to the mall, maybe see a movie?" Frederica gushed.

Honey sat up and stretched, then looked at the cheap watch she'd purchased the day before. Any electronics that relied on signals from somewhere else, like cell phones, went haywire in and around the school, but simple watches worked fine, or so Frederica had informed her.

"Well first I'm going to eat, then I'm going to church, then I'd like to go on a long run. After that, I'm going to read. I have a lot to catch up on."

"Church?"

"Yeah. There are a lot of nice churches around here." Honey held up one of the maps she'd printed off the day before. "I'm going to try one each Sunday."

"Oh." Frederica's face fell.

"You can come. You probably won't want to run with me though, unless you like to run?"

"But churches don't like witches."

"They won't know we're witches. Besides, we aren't like the witches that are mentioned in the Bible. They weren't real witches." Probably. There were a lot of things in the Bible, like the way they treated women, that didn't work in today's society, but the core faith was sound and she always felt at peace when she was in church. God knew what she was and he approved, else she wouldn't exist. Plus, she felt closer to her parents when she was there.

"Come with me. You should try it once at least. I'll explain everything."

Frederica chewed on her lip. It was the first time Honey had seen her anything less than enthusiastic.

"Or don't. That's fine. I go by myself all the time. You have exams coming up, right, and homework?"

"Yeah."

"You should study. I'll study with you when I get back from my run."

"But it's raining."

"I love running in the rain. Besides, it might not be raining by then." And if she didn't get rid of some excess energy it might be more than her claws making an appearance if she got mad again.

"How far are you going to go, a kilometer?" Frederica sounded like she might actually be considering running with her.

Canadians spoke in kilometers. That was going to take some getting used to. Honey quickly did the calculations in her head. A 5K was about three miles, so ten miles would be... "15 or 20 at least. It won't take long," she quickly said at Frederica's crestfallen look. "I'm fast." She folded up the blankets Frederica had located for her so she wouldn't have to buy one at the thrift store and stuffed them inside the pillowcase with the pillow that Frederica had taken off her own bed. She had two, so Honey didn't feel like she was imposing.

Frederica's roommates had been nice enough to say hi when Frederica introduced her. After that, though, they had ignored them both, not even asking why Honey needed a pillow. It was no wonder Frederica was a little clingy.

Honey hugged the stuffed pillowcase to her chest and shot Frederica a smile. "Come on, let's get some breakfast. I'm starving."

"You're always starving."

"Not true." Just only when she had to wrap herself in an air shield all day. She had no idea what the wolf situation was in London. It was about half the size of Indianapolis with fields all around, so there might be a lot of wolves.

She tucked the pillow with her duffel bag in the closest she'd found yesterday just outside the library. One shelf held cleaning supplies, but most of the other shelves hosted dust-covered items that Honey sensed were magical but not what they did. She doubted anyone would notice her things on the now dust-free top shelf.

After a wet walk to and from church, Honey sloshed into the closet, changed into a pair of shorts and the running top her grandmother had insisted she buy new, and switched hats to the one she'd purchased yesterday with a big, generic Canadian leaf on the front. She also wound her braid into a bun. It was mostly her face she was trying to hide from any cameras, but hiding her hair would help. Maybe she should cut it, or even color it. No, that was probably overkill. Lots of people had brown hair. There was no indication that anyone other than Gaian was looking for her anyway. Still, it was too bad Sabine wasn't there, not that she'd be eager to color Honey's hair. Thinking of her friends sent a pang of homesickness slicing through her stomach. She couldn't think about them. She had to focus on what she could do here – learn more about her magic and maybe how to break Zavier's curse.

The water pelting her skin was cold at first, but after the first mile it felt good. She followed the trail up the river to the first bridge, then ran north to the university. Few schools had the wolf and witch populations that Vindale U. did. She likely wouldn't be able to tell if this school had supernatural programs, but it wouldn't hurt to look around.

After a side trip into a wooded area that she was nearly certain was wolf property based on the scents and the two wolf guys she'd passed on the trail going suspiciously slow, she finally made it to the campus. It looked nice enough and felt very spacious with the light-colored buildings, some of them quite old-looking, set back off the roads, but it wasn't Vindale. Still, with pack lands so close, it probably did have wolves and perhaps witches. Maybe there was even a magical library. She'd have to ask Ms. Charming.

At a park she'd marked as a landmark on the map in her head, she turned and ran east until she reached the dojo she wanted to check out. It wasn't that close to the witch school, but the distance would mean the witches might not find out about her skills and she'd have an alternative way to keep her energetic wolf side happy.

Did Canadian colleges have a wolf Olympics?

She didn't even have to go in the building to smell the wolves – a different pack from the one near the college. The dojo was probably wolf-run. There was no way they wouldn't think something was odd if a witch with skills like hers showed up. She quickly altered her course to jog past on the opposite side of the street. Maybe she could take her charm off and be a wolf occasionally. No. Someone had already found her once. If whoever Gaian hired to come after her again did any research at all, they'd know she was a good fighter. They'd be checking all the wolf-run dojos. There had to be someplace that catered only to humans somewhere. Her dad had always managed to find human-only places for her to take classes.

Would the wolves find it suspicious if she asked? She shelved that idea as a last resort.

Since she was in the neighborhood, she decided to swing by the climbing center that was a few blocks to the south over a series of railroad tracks. It wasn't as good an option as a dojo, but she could at least work on her upper-arm strength. She knew it was unlikely that she'd ever get to do an obstacle course against wolves again, but she couldn't squelch the idea that everything would work out by the end of the summer and she'd be able to go back to college with her friends.

The climbing center was bright with fun colors both outside and inside and even better, the center smelled entirely human when she stepped in. A dark-skinned girl with well-defined arms greeted her before she made it past the industrial mat at the entrance.

"Can I help you?"

The girl offered a friendly smile despite all the water pouring off Honey and pooling on the mat.

Honey pulled up her brightest smile. "Yes. I'm new in town. I was running by, and I thought I'd check this place out. Sorry I'm getting your floor all wet. I was going to ask for a tour, but probably not the best idea." She waved at herself. "Do you have a price list or something?"

"Students are $20 for a day or $69 for a month." Her lips twitched. "You should be dry."

Honey pulled up a laugh. "Yes. I figured that."

There was a gym! She could hear the weights. Maybe this *would* work until she could find a dojo. "Does a job come with a membership?"

"Yes."

"Any job openings?" She couldn't afford $70 unless she had a job, and it would be even better if she didn't have to afford it.

"Always. You can apply online."

"Excellent. Thank you." She looked down at her puddle. "Sorry for this. I didn't realize it would be so bad."

"How far have you run?"

"At least ten miles I think. I love the rain."

"American?"

"Yes."

The girl nodded with an amused smile. "I'll be seeing you."

9

MEET VICTORIA

The rain stopped about the same time Honey made it to the school. She took off her hat and shook off the water before she stepped inside. Ms Charming was waiting for her. "Isabelle, there you are! My goodness, why are you all wet and where are your clothes?"

"I went for a run and these are my running clothes."

Ms. Charming looked her up and down, "Well in Canada, we usually don't show that much skin."

Honey looked down at her running bra. It wasn't skimpy, but it did leave her belly showing. "I usually don't either, but I knew everything was going to get wet."

Ms. Charming waved her hand, and Honey was suddenly dry, even her shoes.

"Thank you."

Ms. Charming gave her a little nod then waved at the shorter woman next to her. "This is Miss Evelstone. She teaches magical history, magic theory, and spell-crafting. I want you to sit in on her history and theory classes and assist her in her spell-crafting classes for the next couple of weeks. As an assistant, that means you'll be helping her prepare for classes and be on hand in the event she needs you."

"Sounds fun," Honey said honestly.

Young, petite Miss Evelstone flashed a bright smile. "I'm impressed Isabelle. I run too, but I can never seem to get myself out the door when it rains. If I had a body like that, I'd probably put in more effort. I don't think I've ever seen a girl with a six-pack."

"Thank you."

"Yes, well, go take a shower and put on some clothes," Ms. Charming said, keeping her eyes up. "Afterward, Miss Evelstone can you give a tour of her classroom. Her office is just down the hall from mine."

The problem with storing her clothes in a closet next to the library off the entry hall was that everyone around noticed when she opened the door in the middle of the day. Luckily, Ms. Charming and Miss Evelstone had gone their separate ways after meeting with her. She dragged her duffel bag down off the top shelf and headed for the stairs.

Frederica was coming down at the same time. "You're back. I was starting to get worried. Did you have a good run?"

"I did."

"How far did you go?"

"Not sure. Did you get your homework done?"

"Move it losers."

Frederica shrank into herself and moved to the side. Honey looked up onto the face of a girl who looked almost identical to Frederica except for the nasty sneer and the smell. Frederica smelled like a cement tunnel. Victoria, because who else could it be, smelled like – wool? Honey wasn't quite sure how to describe it.

Honey looked at her friend. "Are you twins?"

"No. She's one year older than me."

Honey stuck out her hand because it was the polite thing to do, and because she wanted to see how Victoria would react.

"Victoria, hi. I'm H..Isabelle."

Victoria sneered down at Honey's outstretched hand. "Well, Hisabelle, you are in the way. Move."

"I would but you and your friends are blocking the stairs. If you would all kindly move to your right, Frederica and I will move to ours and we will all be able to go where we were going."

Victoria stood straighter and would have probably puffed up like an alpha if she had that power – a miniature alpha. She was lucky she was two steps above Honey or she would've been below eye-level.

"I hear you're new, so maybe you don't know the rules. I'm an upperclassman. You are beneath me. You are beneath all of us. That means what we say," she waved her finger around at her friends, "goes."

"Actually, I'm a sophomore, *in College*. I find your rules silly and immature. Just step to the right like normal people and I'll forget this happened."

"Liar."

Honey removed her duffel bag from her shoulder and offered it to her friend. "Frederica, would you hold my bag please?"

Frederica looked at her with wide eyes, but took the bag. Victoria took her hand out of her pocket and opened it under Honey's face. Honey caught a glimpse of a circle of gray right before a red ball of sparks formed.

"You touch me, I'll burn you."

"Pretty." Honey froze everything but Victoria's head and picked her up and moved her over. The sparkling red ball neither grew nor shrank, so she didn't bother disabling the charm that was powering it. "Do the rest of you need help going to the right, or are you good?"

The three girls behind Victoria shuffled to the side. "Thank you. Come on Frederica."

"Wait! What did you do to me?" Victoria demanded.

Honey waited until they'd passed the girls and Frederica was above her on the stairs before she turned around and released Victoria's molecules. "What are you talking about?"

The ball of sparks abruptly expanded. Honey threw an air shield across the stairs just in time to beat the explosion. She and Frederica were fine, but everything within a five-foot radius of Victoria's hand looked singed, including Victoria's clothes.

"I definitely didn't do that," Honey said.

"Victoria Felix, my office. Now!"

Perhaps because she was in shock, Victoria meekly obeyed Ms. Charming and stumbled down the stairs to the office without throwing any threats back at her sister. Her friends slunk down the stairs and went a different way. Once she was certain they were gone, Honey took her bag back from a wide-eyed Frederica.

"Thanks for holding my bag."

"How did you do that?"

"What, move her? I lift weights. She was pretty light."

"No," she waved her hand vaguely in the air, "control her power."

"I didn't. That was all her."

Frederica snickered. "She is going to be in so much trouble. We're not supposed to do magic in the halls or on the stairs."

Oops.

"Is there a list of rules somewhere?"

Frederica snickered again.

10

A CHARMING MONDAY

Miss Evelstone taught a total of four classes: Magical History I, Magical Theory II, Spell-crafting 1a and Spell-crafting 1b. Spell-crafting 1a took place at 8 am in the morning while spell-crafting 1b took place after lunch to give plenty of time to clean up from the morning class. After meeting with Miss Evelstone, Honey spent the rest of Sunday and well into the night reading the spell-crafting book Miss Evelstone loaned her. Mom had taught her bits and pieces here and there but having it all together was nice. Honey had her pillow back in the closet by 6:30 am, ate breakfast, then ran upstairs to the third floor to retrieve her toiletry bag from a different closet and brush her teeth. The lesson for today was basic charm-making and she didn't want to miss it.

There were two kinds of charms: spelled and magicked. Spelled charms were items that had a spell put on them to perform a function, like keeping water hot. They were always on until they wore out and easy to make if you could cast spells. Magicked charms trapped the caster's innate magic and held the magic until it was released. They were harder because you had to direct your magic into the charm and convince it to stay. Honey was hoping to try and capture her ability to freeze things. It would be a useful self-defense charm.

She didn't get a chance to try during either of the classes. Too many people needed help or more ingredients or a trip to the healer. It was crazy. It was a chemistry class gone horribly wrong. It was like giving a bunch of pre-schoolers firecrackers and matches, telling them to drop the firecrackers into the bottles, then figure out how to light them with whatever craft supplies they could find. Honey wished she was taking the class instead of helping with it.

Miss Evelstone came up to Honey after the second class while she was wiping some mysterious pink liquid off a table. Why someone would want a charm filled with pink goo was beyond her. Miss Evelstone had a dark streak across her cheekbone and it looked like part of her hair had been singed off, but she was smiling.

"What did you think, eh?"

Honey shook her head. "I have no words."

Miss Evelstone threw back her head and laughed. She had a great laugh. "Mondays are always messy. I like to give the students a chance to try the spells after they read the theory. They tend to pay more attention to the details after they fail. It won't be this wild on Wednesday. You read over the lesson, right?"

"Yes."

"Why don't you give it a go?"

"Right now?"

"Yeah."

Honey eagerly grabbed a small pendant out of the pile of ones that hadn't melted. Charms could be activated by breaking them, which was easiest; touching them; by voice; or by touch and voice. It was safest to use touch and voice to make sure you didn't accidentally set the charm off and that it worked on your target and not yourself. They were also the hardest to make.

She knew the theory and she'd watched her mom make them a few times. She'd even tried once or twice under her mom's supervision without success. She thought she understood now, though. She had to build and bind the spell in her mind before she applied it to the charm.

She pictured her command as a bright blue ball of power, wrapped it in shining gold threads, tied them together with a bow, then put the pendant to her lips. Blowing, she pictured her gift-wrapped power flowing into the charm and mumbled 'freeze dirt-bag' right before she pulled the pendant away.

The charm didn't explode or melt and the spell didn't immediately leak out. She could see it inside the pendant. She handed it to Miss Evelstone.

"Want to test it on me?"

The teacher didn't even hesitate to take it from her. The woman was brave.

"What does it do?"

"It should freeze me for thirty-seconds. It's for self-defense."

"Ah, well, you should never test your own charms on yourself, especially freezing charms because you need to be able to move in case something goes wrong. I made that mistake the first time I made a freeze-stone. I was stuck there for hours before my mom found me. Does it only work on people?"

"No. You made a freeze-stone?"

"It's my family's business. We put all kinds of charms on stones, thus my surname. Someone in the past took issue with our business and called us 'Evil stone' or maybe 'those evil stone-makers'. Thankfully, it got shortened to 'Evelstone'." She waved Honey's charm around. "Let's clean-up, then we'll go for a walk and find something to test this on, like a squirrel. I can't wait to try that release phrase on those evil little pesky varmints." She finished with a low growl under her breath.

Honey snickered. Miss Evelstone was about as scary as a kitten.

"What do you have against squirrels?"

"Do have a couple of days?"

In the end they found a park full of flowers and bees. Miss Evelstone froze a particularly persistent bumble bee that fell out of the air and landed at her feet. Thirty seconds later, it shook itself and flew away. She did not freeze herself, nor did she freeze any other bees.

"Impressive that I was able to target a specific bee," Miss Evelstone said, tossing Honey the now-empty charm. "Of course, if you were to market it, you'd have to test how close a person has to be to their target, how long the charm lasts if you wear it and don't use it, whether it is possible to use it on more than one person at once, etc."

"Does your family make a freezing charm?"

"Not like that. We trend toward freeze stones, shields, and anti-magic devices."

"Like the inhibitors the Enforcers use?"

"How did you know about that?"

"I saw them make an arrest once."

"Yep, that's us."

"Wow. The school is lucky to have you."

"Eh, I didn't see myself whispering spells into stones all day. I'd rather have random spells shot at me from a roomful of fledgling witches." She patted the crunchy, blackened hair on the side of her head with a grin. "Better than a gray streak."

After they got back, Honey went to the public library near the shopping center and looked up how to apply for a job at the climbing place. It was more challenging than she expected. She'd never made a resume before and there wasn't really much she could say. Several hours later, after a kind librarian had given her some tips and read it over, Honey sent it off. It felt like she was throwing a fledgling bird up into the air and hoping it figured out how to fly before it crashed.

11

ONE WEEK LATER

Every day after classes that week and the beginning of the next, Honey checked the email account she'd set up at the public library. She wasn't the only witch student who frequented the library, but most students had phones and went elsewhere to check their accounts. Frederica had a phone, but she tended to tag along with Honey. Honey didn't mind. Frederica was sweet, and Honey didn't like the way Victoria eyed them and whispered to her friends whenever they passed. She was certain Victoria was planning some kind of revenge and she didn't want Frederica to have to face it alone.

Tuesday afternoon the email she'd been waiting for finally arrived. Crossing her fingers, she clicked on it. The climbing center wanted her to come by!

"Yes!"

The quiet murmurs from the other visitors in the library fell silent. Oops.

"What?" Frederica whispered beside her.

"They want to interview me." Honey whispered back, doing her best to act like the outburst had not come from her. "They're open tonight until ten. I could go now."

"Maybe I should go with you?"

"It's about two miles away. That's over three kilometers. I'm going to run. You sure you want to come?"

Frederica curled her nose. "You're going to be all sweaty when you get there."

"It's a gym. Besides, I can just pop in the restroom and clean up a little first." She pulled up a map and memorized the directions again. "I'm going back to school and change."

Frederica shut her schoolbook. "I'll come with you."

"Are you sure. It's nice and quiet in here."

"Yeah, but there are no snacks."

Frederica's bag was full of snacks, but Honey didn't point that out. "I suppose you can come to the climbing place if you want. We can walk." She had already gone for a run before class this morning. This time she'd run east on the south side of the Thames River. As she suspected that territory belonged to yet another wolf pack. They'd left their scent all along the trail and she'd seen a couple of 'park police' that she was certain were also wolves. That was three packs so far. They seemed to be using the rivers as their borders, at least in downtown London. She had already picked another waterway for her next long run so she could test her hypothesis.

"Okay," Frederica said, interrupting Honey's thoughts.

The cool morning had morphed into a beautiful, warm, late spring day. Honey listened to Frederica's constant stream of chatter with one ear while checking out their surroundings. If she got the job, this was the path she'd take to get there. It was picturesque and populated solely by humans as far as her nose could tell.

She got the job.

It wasn't quite the one she was hoping for. Event staff positions didn't come with gym memberships, but she managed to convince the manager to let her have one just at that site for as long as she worked there. Her first day was this Saturday, 9 am. She dearly wished she could tell the guys. They'd be impressed, or act like it anyway.

Frederica still had two more days of finals so Honey quizzed her on magical theory while they walked back to the school. The last day of classes, Thursday, coincided with the full moon. The whole school was going on a field trip outside of town to celebrate the end of the year under the light of the full moon. It would be Honey's first-ever coven meeting. She hoped it went better than her first pack run.

After saying goodnight to Frederica and her roommates, who were slowly becoming friendlier, Honey hoisted the backpack Frederica had given her onto her shoulders and started downstairs. It reminded her of leaving the boy's dorm in the evening, but usually one or more of them had escorted her out. What were the boys doing? Had they found jobs? Were they going camping this weekend? Had they received their grades yet?

Perhaps if she hadn't been daydreaming about making s'mores, she would have noticed someone sneaking up on her. She'd just started down the stairs to the second floor when a hard force slammed into her back from behind. She fell face-first, but because she was falling, she had extra time to decide how to place her hands and gauge if she had enough speed to stick a landing at the bottom of the stairs. She landed on a tread with both hands and launched herself into a front flip with a twist so that she landed facing back up the stairs.

Victoria gaped at her from the top of the stairs. After a moment, she shook the dumbfounded look off her face and planted her hands on her hips with a sassy smirk. The two girls behind her belatedly copied her actions.

"Why did you do that?" Honey asked.

"You can't prove it was me."

She'd wanted Honey hurt and now she wanted a confrontation. Not happening. Honey shrugged and turned her back on the three. "Okay."

"Wait!"

Honey ignored her and started down the next flight.

"Loser!"

Should she be concerned for Frederica?

"Isabelle is a loser! Isabelle is a loser!"

Victoria was really trying hard to make her mad. Why? Honey had read the rules. No fighting was allowed anywhere, and no spells in the hall or on the stairs. Did she want to be punched? Oh, maybe she was trying to catch something on camera so Honey would get kicked out. She'd tell the girl to give it up and go to bed, but it wasn't worth it.

"Look at the loser, running away."

Honey snorted. Victoria sounded like she was reading one of those 'See Dick, See Jane' stories from the old book her mom had picked up from a garage sale once.

"Loser, loser, lonely, lonely loser."

Great, Victoria was getting louder, which meant the girl was following her. Victoria was a bully, but Honey hadn't thought she was stupid until now. The teachers took turns roaming at night. One of them was going to hear her. Honey glanced up at her reflection in a dark window to judge how close Victoria was. Oddly, the girl was still on the stairs, nowhere near as close as she sounded. Had she somehow spelled Honey so that only she could hear the taunting? She couldn't smell anything, well, except the residue of the thousands of spells that had been cast over the years.

Maybe Victoria hadn't meant to push her down the stairs. Maybe she'd had a different goal.

Honey slipped her backpack off and around. A literal bug that looked like a decorative pin an old lady would wear on a scarf had been jabbed into the front pocket. Honey sniffed at it. Halitosis. Nasty. She pulled it off and dropped it into one of the potted plants in the entry hall.

"Honey, where are you going?"

She spun around with a smile ready. "Evening Ms. Charming. Just going to the library."

"Again?"

"That's where all the books are."

"It's nearly curfew."

"I know. Reading helps me sleep sometimes."

"Well, hurry." Ms. Charming looked around. "What is that noise?"

She frowned down at the plant then bent and plucked the bug up out of the soil. She put it next to her ear, then quickly pulled it away with a very severe look on her face. "Excuse me."

"Of course."

Phooey, now Ms. Charming would check the library on her next round. Honey really needed to find a better place to sleep, but it was only for a few more days.

As usual, no one else was in the library. The students all preferred to study in their rooms or in the cushy chairs and window seats in the lounges upstairs. Honey jogged up the spiral staircase that led to the top level of the three-story tower. She was fairly certain Ms. Charming wouldn't bother going all the way up, especially if Honey didn't use a light.

She didn't need one tonight. The nearly full moon directly above the skylight gave off more than enough light for her to read by. She sat on the window seat she'd been thrilled to discover and pulled out the "How to Go Invisible" book she'd purchased at a used bookstore during one of her runs. She'd picked it up thinking humans had accidentally found a book on magic but discovered it was all about keeping one's identity private online and in the world. She'd been dearly tempted to send her friends an email when she signed up for a new account in the library, but after reading part of the book, she was glad she hadn't. Gaian was still out there and someone had already found her once. Her friends would be closely monitored, likely by both magic and technology. Spies sent secret messages all the time though, at least in the movies. There had to be a way that she could communicate with the guys without getting herself or them into trouble.

12

TO SAVE A ROGUE

The bonfire was everything Honey had imagined it would be and more. First of all, it was huge. All the witches from the school were able to fit around it. It was a little like the bonfires the wolves had with all the laughing and drinking and eating, but wolves didn't usually dance without music or set off random spells and send up magical sparks. She wished the guys were there. She could just imagine Nathan flirting with Frederica and Luca trying to make everyone laugh. Liam would be sitting beside her, silently observing while Walter would be one spot down, conjuring up some profound comment that she wouldn't realize the depth of until days later. Why had they never invited their witch friends to share a bonfire on a full moon? They should. It would be a blast. The witches could do their thing while the wolves went for a run, then they could all sit around and watch the embers die together, maybe while telling ghost stories.

"What are you thinking?" Frederica asked.

Honey shook her head. "I was wondering if we're going to tell ghost stories."

"I doubt it."

"No," Stacy, another girl Honey had befriended said from her other side. "They'll give out awards tonight, all except the ones for Grade 12. They'll give those out at graduation tomorrow."

"What are you doing for the summer Stacy," Honey asked. "Are you coming back here?"

"No. My mom and I are going to tour Europe."

"I'd like to do that someday," Frederica sighed wistfully.

"I think of everyone here, you are the most likely to travel," Honey said.

"Yeah, if my magic ever comes in."

Not knowing what else to do, Honey patted her on the back. "It will."

A lone howl pierced the air. Shortly after, a full chorus of wolves joined in. Honey itched to join them, but that would be an excellent way to get caught.

"Why do they do that," Stacy asked, looking nervously over her shoulder.

"It's a rally call of sorts," Honey said automatically, then covered with, "I googled it once."

"I don't understand why they run. It's dark. They could hurt themselves," Frederica stated.

"Wolves have good night vision, and with the moon out, it's pretty bright. Wouldn't you run if you had four legs and could see in the dark?"

"No."

Honey snorted. Frederica's hatred of exercise was extreme.

"It sounds like they're getting closer," Stacy said, chewing her lip and looking over her shoulder toward the sound again.

"I doubt they'll try anything. It doesn't sound like there's a lot of them. I think we have them outnumbered. Together, we can easily take them," Honey said truthfully.

"Maybe you guys can," Frederica grumped.

Honey elbowed her. "Cheer up. We'll protect you, and then when your power does come in, you can take us *all* to Europe."

The wolves were close enough she could hear them growling under their pants now. This was not a fun run, and they were headed directly toward them.

"Ladies, to me. Form a circle. Those of you who know defensive spells form the outer ring. The rest of you will make up the center." It sounded like she was talking right into Honey's ear, but Honey could clearly see Ms. Charming on the other side of the fire, glowing. All the girls immediately got up to their feet and flowed toward her, oddly calm.

Honey leaned toward Frederica. "Has everyone been spelled or have you guys practiced this?"

"Practiced, every full moon. We all have designated spots depending on our skills. I'm always right at the center," she sighed.

"Which is exactly where you'll be once your power comes in. You'll be able to help everyone escape," Honey said.

"Oh."

"Isabelle, you're with me," Miss Evelstone called. She leaned closer once Honey was beside her. "How many people can you freeze at once?"

"I don't know," Honey said honestly.

"We might be about to find out."

The wolves ran close enough to be seen. A thin, scruffy one was running as fast as he could in front of a small pack of sleek, healthy-looking beasts. Barely forty feet away from their circle, one of the wolves behind the scruffy one managed to claw his hind leg. The lead wolf yelped and faltered and was immediately surrounded. A big wolf, whom Honey pegged as the alpha, pushed his way into the circle to tower over the scrawny wolf. The wolf holding the first one down stepped back with his head bowed. The alpha flipped the scrawny wolf over, at least that was what it looked like from where Honey was standing. It didn't sound like the scrawny wolf was fighting, just panting frantically because he knew those were the last breaths he'd ever take.

She couldn't let them kill him. He wanted to live. She broke out of the circle and ran closer. "Wait! What are you doing?"

"Isabelle, get back here," Ms. Charming commanded.

"Are you going to kill him? What has he done?" Honey screamed.

"Isabelle!"

One of the larger wolves on the edge of the circle surrounding the other two looked back at her and started to transform. He was fast. It only took him about twenty seconds. "Stay back witch. This is wolf business."

"What has he done?"

"He is a rogue. We caught him stealing in our territory. It is our right to punish him."

"You are going to kill him," she stated.

"He has been a rogue a long time. There is no other option."

She stepped closer, partially so the witches behind her couldn't hear and said softly. "I might be an option."

"What?"

"Let me look into his head. Maybe I can help."

"We're not going to let a witch into his head."

"You'd rather cut it off?" she challenged. "Give me a chance. Give him a chance."

"He won't have anywhere to go even if you can help him."

"You could take him into your pack."

"No," a deep voice came from inside the circle. A big man climbed to his feet. Honey kept her eyes up. "Get out of here, little witch, you are interfering with pack business."

"Why won't you accept him into your pack?"

"He's trouble."

"May I talk to him?"

He lifted his chin towards the witches behind her. "Get back to your circle."

"Please. I know some wolves. I know one who might take him in. It's far away from here. Do you truly want to kill someone tonight? Let me talk to him."

"You're wasting everyone's time."

She waved her arm at the bright circle in the sky. "The moon isn't going anywhere, well, not quickly."

The alpha shook his head and kicked the wolf on the ground, but not hard. "Transform."

It was slow, but in a few minutes, a naked, dirty teenager was laying on the ground in front of her. He was so skinny Honey could count all his ribs. She wanted to hug him and then give him pizza. How could anyone want to hurt him? She took off her hoodie and knelt down to cover him with it. Behind her she could hear Ms. Charming arguing with someone. She didn't have much time.

"Hi. I'm Isabelle. How long have you been a rogue?"

"Years."

"Why?"

He shook his head. "I ran away. Our alpha was a bad man. I couldn't stay."

"Did you try to find another pack?"

"No. I didn't want to go right back to the same situation."

"May I look inside your head?"

He looked up at her for the first time. "Why?"

"I might be able to help."

He shook his head. "The witches all say no one can help. It is the curse of the wolf."

"Every witch has different powers. Just because none of them could help doesn't mean I can't. I just want to look. I'll ask before I try anything. We have to hurry though before Ms. Charming gets here."

He studied her face while she studied his. His hair was scraggly and long and his cheekbones and chin too sharp for someone his age. Her heart ached for him. He nodded after a moment. She wasted no time pushing her fingers into his greasy hair. Some of his molecules weren't moving at all. It was like a whole portion of his brain was frozen. Looking deeper, she saw why. The fluid between them was solid and it looked like it was spreading.

"I see it. I think I can help. Will you let me try?"

"Sure, why not?"

She'd pulled up her air shield as soon as they'd heard wolves so they wouldn't smell her 'I'm a witch' charm, but would that cause a problem when they couldn't smell her magic? She didn't have time to figure out how to make just part of her scent leak through. She'd have to work on that later.

She concentrated on getting the boy's molecules moving again in the hopes that it would loosen up the gunk in-between. To her relief, it was a lot easier to set them spinning than she anticipated, much easier than trying to convince them to spin in opposite directions like she had in Zavier's head after his had gotten all messed up from drinking cursed beer. She made the molecules wobble a little too, to get the fluid around them to start moving.

"There," she said finally, pulling her fingers away. She felt a little tired, like she'd run up a really big hill, but not nearly as drained as forty-five minutes in Zavier's head. "How's that?"

"I feel, good."

"Good." She carefully looked up to the alpha, who was looming naked as a plucked chicken above them with his arms crossed over his hairy chest. "I don't know how long that will last if he stays outside a pack. Why don't you give him a chance," she dropped her eyes to the teen, "give each other a chance. I'm sure you've heard stories about all the packs around here. Is he a bad alpha?"

The boy shook his head. "Not from what I've heard."

She looked the alpha in the eye. "He's just a boy. You can always put him down if my fix doesn't work. And you," she turned again to the boy, "can come to me if he's not a good alpha. I'll tell you how to reach my friend."

"I'm willing if he is," the teen said.

"That's not how this works," the alpha growled. "What did you do to him, witch?"

"I…" were witches supposed to know about telepathy? "Part of his part of his brain was frozen. It looked like it was spreading. I loosened it up. It's not a cure, but maybe if he is part of a pack, it won't freeze up again."

The alpha contemplated the boy. "How old are you?"

"Fifteen."

The alpha sighed. He was going to accept him, she was sure of it.

"I'll leave you two to figure it out." She rocked back on her heels so she could stand.

"Wait." The boy took a deep sniff of her hoodie. She didn't keep up the air shield in the school. Could he smell the lie from the charm or her wolf? He didn't act like he smelled anything odd. He just gave her a cocky little smile before he handed her hoodie back. "So I can find you."

"Hopefully you won't need to."

"What if I want to?"

She could see the alpha shaking his head out of the corner of her eye.

"I live in a school with hundreds of other witches who formed a defensive circle when they saw you guys coming. I wouldn't recommend it." She stood and bowed her head to the alpha, keeping her eyes averted. "Thank you for listening."

She turned away from him, only to come face-to-face with Ms. Charming who was standing with her hands on her hips next to the first man who had transformed. "Isabelle, get back in the circle."

Honey bowed to her too.

13

PIZZA PARTIES

Honey took her place by Miss Evelstone, who raised an eyebrow at her before turning her attention back to the wolves. The three wolves transformed and then ran off together with the rest of the pack in the direction from which they came. Honey didn't see the alpha accept the boy into his pack, but he might have done it when she was walking back to the circle. The witches remained in their circle, whispering and giggling until Ms. Charming announced, "You may return to what you were doing. Isabelle, walk with me. Miss Evelstone, please join us."

"I can't believe you did that." Frederica whispered behind Honey. "You are so brave."

Honey shrugged and moved closer to Ms. Charming as requested.

Ms. Charming didn't look upset while she and Miss Evelstone approached, but Honey could smell her anger. Ms. Charming waved a finger in some kind of signal to one of the other teachers, then turned her back on the fire and started walking away from it.

"What did you wish to speak about?" Honey asked when Ms. Charming didn't say anything after at least ten steps.

Ms. Charming spun around and got right in her face. "What were you thinking?"

"About what?"

"You left the protective circle and approached a pack of angry wolves. You could have gotten us into a fight. Some of the girls could have been hurt or killed."

"I was thinking I didn't want to see anyone murdered."

"It was a wolf," Ms. Charming snapped.

"It was a person."

"We aren't allowed to interrupt their proceedings."

"If they had refused to listen, I would have backed away. I had to try."

"And then you healed him."

"No. I just unlocked his brain temporarily."

"Witches aren't allowed to help rogues. It's forbidden."

"By who?"

"By the witch council."

"Really? I didn't know."

Ms. Charming sighed. "From what Miss Evelstone tells me, you are not a healer. What did you do to that boy?"

Honey hadn't told Miss Evelstone much about her powers, so she assumed Ms. Charming was talking about the freezing charm. "When I freeze people, I make their molecules go still. I had a feeling his problem had something to do with his molecules so I took a look. Part of his brain looked like he had a bunch of marbles stuck in syrup. I made them move again."

"His molecules?" Miss Evelstone asked.

"It's just the way I picture whatever it is I see inside of people."

"No organs?"

"Nope."

"So I'm just a walking jar of marbles?"

"Basically."

Miss Evelstone snorted.

"Isabelle, so far I've been impressed by your hard work and diligence," Ms. Charming said. "You are new to us, so you don't know how the circle works, but if you ever endanger my students like that again, you are gone."

"I wouldn't have left the circle if they were in danger. There weren't that many wolves and I knew you and Miss Evelstone and the other teachers could stop them. I also knew they were chasing something or someone and weren't targeting us."

"How could you know that?"

"I had a wolf friend growing up. Their howls mean different things."

"Nevertheless, it could have gone bad."

Honey ducked her head. "I'm sorry for causing you to worry."

Ms. Charming huffed a sigh. "Just don't do it again."

After graduation the next morning, most of the students moved out, including Frederica. She didn't act very excited to go home. Her sister had been expelled after Ms. Charming had found the bug in the pot, so perhaps that was the reason. Frederica did seem happy to see her parents again when they arrived by portal to retrieve her, and eagerly introduced Honey as her friend. Frederica's mom kindly invited her to go home with them until the summer session started. For a moment, Honey regretted finding a job, but she needed a place to work out and keep up her skills and she needed spending money. She very respectfully declined.

That night, for the first time since she'd been kidnapped, Honey slept in a bed. Most of the third floor was empty, and since she didn't trust Jessica to not have booby trapped the room on the second floor, Honey slept in Frederica's room. Not having to worry about falling off a narrow couch was nice, but three bare beds was lonelier than shelves full of books.

Saturday morning, she made it to her first ever job fifteen minutes early. By the time the manager was through with her training though, kids were already pouring through the door. Honey barely had time to grab some leftover pizza from the first birthday party she helped at before the people started arriving for the next one.

She was only scheduled to do two parties, but someone didn't show up, so she helped with the third one, then stayed after to go to the gym and try out one of the more challenging climbing walls. Exhausted, but pleased with the day, she returned to the school and had just reached the stairs when Ms. Charming came rushing out of the hall that led to her office.

"Isabelle, where have you been?"

"I was at work."

"Didn't you see the note I left under your door this morning?"

It took Honey a moment to realize Ms. Charming was referring to the room on the second floor where she was supposed to be sleeping the whole time and not the library or Frederica's room. "No, but I slept up in Frederica's old room. I like the third floor."

"You should have told me you moved up there. I took everyone who is left on a trip to the museum of witchcraft today."

"There's a museum of witchcraft?"

"Yes. Now what's this about work? I don't remember you asking if you could get a job."

"I didn't know I needed to. It's part time and pretty flexible except for Saturdays. They definitely need me on Saturdays."

"What are you doing?"

"Event staff," Honey grinned. "I got a job at a climbing center where people can rent space to throw parties."

"A climbing center?"

"Yeah, it's like rock climbing except it's indoors and they have pieces of plastic that look like rocks screwed into the walls so you can climb them."

"People do that?"

"Yeah. I helped with three birthday parties today."

"Where is this place?"

Honey told her and the name and how she was going to get there and gave her the phone number for the place in case she needed to call her at work. She also agreed to inform her when she had to go in. She didn't mind. Ms.

Charming was just trying to do her job and it was nice to have someone to tell.

14

ALONE

By Monday, Honey was the only student left and would be for the next two weeks until summer camp started. Most of the teachers left too. She hadn't interacted with many people while they were there, but the quiet emptiness of the building weighed on her. She couldn't keep the tears at bay past the second night.

She let herself have a good cry, then, after a stern self-scolding, emerged from her empty room to take full advantage of the excellent opportunity her grandmother had provided. She finally had access to magical books and ingredients and instructors, and nothing to get in the way of learning. If she focused and learned two spells a day instead of a spell a week, she'd be able to condense two of Miss Evelstone's 14-week courses into two weeks.

Tuesday afternoon, Ms. Charming called her into the office and handed Honey a note so the librarian at the university, which did have a program for witches, would let her peruse the texts on abjuration there and even check them out, since the school library was lacking. Honey immediately caught a bus to the college library and along with the abjuration books, found several books on curses

114

and biographies and autobiographies on curse-breakers. Those she only read in the library so no one would know she was researching curses and start asking questions. She was tempted to check out the college's copy of *The Magic of Molecules*, but on the very off chance the librarian in Indianapolis was looking for her and was somehow monitoring library records, she resisted.

She was also still trying to figure out if the wolf/witch hybrid curse was real and if so, where it was. It had to be a written curse to have lasted so long and affected so many people, unless the witches had bathed everyone in blood or made them drink something with blood in it, and she didn't think that was the case. Also, if all the wolves and witches were cursed, why couldn't she see it?

She bought herself a new notebook and wrote all her notes in a modified pigpen cypher that she'd made up when she was eight. That was the year she and her dad had exchanged coded notes every time he visited. Had her bio-dad ever wrote messages in code? She couldn't picture it.

That was when she had a brilliant idea. What if she used code to send her friends a message? They'd talked about secret codes once. Surely one of them would remember her pangram idea. She could use a remailing service like one of the incognito books had suggested! She'd just have to figure out how to pay online anonymously.

The idea sounded even better after sleeping on it. She was on her morning run and imagining how Walter would react if he received a coded message from her when a vice of fingers wrapped around her arm.

She reacted automatically, twisting her arm so she could grab her attacker's wrist and spinning around with her other elbow up to clock her attacker in the face. She made contact, then saw who she'd hit and backed away.

"Sorry, you startled me."

The teenage wolf she'd rescued rubbed his jaw. Two others snorted behind him. "My fault. Probably shouldn't have grabbed you."

He looked a lot better, cleaner anyway. He was still painfully thin. "How's it going? Did the alpha accept you into the pack?"

"Yeah."

"Are these your friends?" She nodded at the two behind him.

"My keepers."

"Oh. Do you mind if I take a look at your head? What I did was a complete experiment. I'm not sure if it will last."

He stepped closer. "Not at all."

She didn't have to touch his head, but he seemed to expect it, so she did. His intense blue-eyed stare was disconcerting. She shut her eyes and made herself concentrate. It only took her about a minute. She dropped her hands and stepped back. "A little sluggish."

She turned to the two watching. "I think it's related to your telepathy. You should take him running in wolf form every night for a while. Find me after a few days and I'll see if it helped."

"You know about that?" the burlier of the two frowned. He wasn't bad looking with his brown curly hair,

116

brown eyes, and the shadow on his chin although she didn't think he'd reached his twenties yet.

"Yeah. I was friends with a wolf when I was younger. Kids share things that maybe adults don't always want them to. Don't worry, I haven't told anyone."

"Can we run with you?" the teen she'd rescued asked.

"I don't think…" the burly one started.

"Sure. What are your names?" Honey interrupted.

"I'm Cede," the teen said, "that's Derrik," he pointed to the slimmer of the two with him, "and Rock," he pointed to the burly one, "and you're Isabelle."

She smiled instead of agreeing. "Think you can keep up? I like to go fast."

"We're wolves."

"Ah, but you are in human form and I'm very fast for a human, unless you want to change first." She raised an eyebrow.

"That won't be necessary," Rock stated firmly.

"Catch me if you can then."

She took off. Rock was the first one to reach her, and he did manage to stay with her for about half a mile, then he dropped back. She kept going, but after they'd fallen so far behind they would never be able to catch her, she had pity on them and slowed to a jog.

"You used magic," Rock accused when they'd caught up with her.

"Did I?"

He sniffed. She knew he wouldn't be able to smell anything. Her ability to hold her shield was getting better with all the practice she'd had recently. He gave her a

117

disgruntled look and she grinned. "I was on the track team last year."

"The witches have a track team?"

"Not that school. So, are you in college or high school Rock?" she asked before he could ask what school she'd attended.

"College. I'll be a sophomore next semester."

"What about you, Derrik?"

"Same."

"At Western?"

"No. Our school is smaller."

"Oh. I know witches go there. I thought wolves would too."

Rock shrugged, "Some do, if that's the only place they can find their major."

She looked at her watch. "I need to turn around. Guess I'll see you guys around."

"We'll go with you," Cede said.

"No," Rock said. "We're supposed to be patrolling."

"How many packs are in London?" Honey asked Rock.

"Three, but downtown is considered neutral territory."

"Between the railroad tracks where the witch school is?" she guessed.

"Yeah. How did you know?"

"I don't run into as many wolves there."

"Be careful of the pack to the south," Cede said. "They aren't nice. You should stick to this territory."

"The ones that dress like cops?"

Cede nodded.

"I don't think they pay attention to humans and they don't know I'm a witch, but thanks for the warning."

Her brief adventure with the wolves made her think of her friends. What it would be like if the guys could visit her in London? Would they like the climbing place? She hadn't tried very many restaurants and definitely no clubs, but maybe they could all find some good ones together. What if she sent them a postcard with a picture of London and signed a random name? Would they recognize her handwriting?

What if someone was checking their mail though? They'd know something was odd. Hardly anyone sent postcards anymore. It would be far safer if she didn't send anything. Then Gaian and whoever he'd hired wouldn't have any clues to follow.

Would it be safe to look her friends up on the web if she used the 'incognito' option in the browser? She wouldn't be able to let them know she was alive and thinking of them, but she could follow when they got their degrees and found wives and… it was really hard to run and cry at the same time. She wanted to be a part of their lives. They already knew what she was. There had to be a way.

15

ANTI-ALPHA HELMET

It was another beautiful morning with a nearly perfect running temperature in the shade even though it was the middle of June. She ran to the fork in the river, then turned onto the trail that went south, then east along the river. Had the boys received her letters and decrypted the code yet? It had been nearly two weeks since she'd sent the message to Walter and the key to Nathan. There were another four days before she'd told them to meet her on the message board. Would they figure out her code in time?

They would. They probably already had.

She turned onto the four-lane bridge with badly cracked asphalt to cross over the river to the short section of trail on the other side. Between the full sun, car exhaust, and run-down state of the place, it wasn't her favorite bridge, but it wasn't that long.

She was almost half-way over when a dog barked behind her and someone yelled, "No. Get back here."

She spun around just in time to see an exuberant wolf with his tongue trailing out of his mouth leap for her. She stepped out of the way at the last moment and his feet landed on the sidewalk behind her instead of her shoulders. He immediately turned around and butted his head against her thigh and then under her hand.

"Cede?" she guessed.

"Yes. He's an idiot," Rock groused, jogging up to them. "Won't listen. He wants you to check his head."

"Why?"

"I think he likes having you in there."

"Um, okay." She dug her fingers into the fur on the top of his head, not because she needed to, but because it was soft and thick and he was pushing his head into her hand, urging her on. "It looks fine."

Cede rubbed his side against her, urging her to pet his back.

"You know all that tail wagging just makes you look desperate," Rock chastised.

"As least he's not afraid to show his emotions," the female wolf with them sniffed.

Rock waved his hand between the two girls. "Isabelle, Hannah, Hannah, Isabelle."

"Witch," Hannah said with a quick nod.

"Wolf," Honey said right back.

Cede ran toward some trees on the side of the bridge she'd just left and looked back, urging her to follow him with his eyes.

"I was going to go over the bridge and run on the trail on the other side of the river."

Cede came back and whined and tried to push her backwards.

"Stop that."

"Miss, is that animal bothering you?"

More wolves, the uniformed kind, with their own guard dog/wolf stood behind her.

"No."

Cede moved in front of her to growl. The other wolf in wolf-form growled back. Honey grabbed the leash dragging behind Cede, then squatted beside him and pushed her fingers into his fur. "Stop."

"Is he yours?"

"He's ours," Rock said. "What are you guys doing here?"

"The bridge is a public place."

Honey interpreted that to mean it was neutral territory. Did that mean all the bridges were? She made a note to ask later. Cede was still growling under his breath and was pushing into her like he wanted to push her back to his side. It probably *was* a good idea to get him back in his pack's territory.

She stepped back, pulling Cede with her. "Come on silly, but I'm not going to race you. You'll beat me."

"Race? You want to have a race, eh? Come here boy." One of the uniformed men tapped on his leg.

Cede growled.

"You sure that's not a wild dog? He doesn't seem very well trained," the young man taunted. His face and his voice grew stern. "I said come here!"

Cede whimpered. He was fighting it, but she could see the jerk in his stupid uniform growing with alpha power. If she wasn't...wait...she was a witch now, not that the bullies would be able to tell with the breeze and her air shield but Cede already knew. Would one of her new skills work? She envisioned the molecules in the air sticking and molding together to form a solid shield around Cede's head. He straightened from the hunched position he'd been in and gave her an inquisitive look. She raised her eyebrows. He grinned and his tongue lolled out like he was laughing.

She squatted and rubbed Cede's head around his ears like he really was a dog. "You're such a good boy. You know better than to talk to strangers."

He licked her right up the middle of her face.

"Ugh. That's just gross." She stood to get away from his tongue and scrubbed her face with her running shirt. "You two coming or am I kidnapping your dog?"

The young man in the uniform deflated, his well-formed face ruined with a nasty expression. Rock and Hannah straightened and turned with smiles as if she truly were human and they hadn't just been crushed under the weight of the jerk's power.

"Sure," Rock said. "Last one off the bridge has to run with the dog, and he stops and sniffs at everything."

Honey was not the last one off the bridge. Hannah won that distinction, much to her irritation. Honey kept going until they reached a secluded part of the path without any ears around, then stopped and started stretching. "What pack was that? You don't seem to have a very cordial relationship."

Rock snorted. "That's one way of putting it."

"I'm guessing that jerk who was bossing Cede around was an alpha or a beta's son?"

"One of the alpha's son," Hannah responded. "Thinks he's special."

"Cede wants to know what you did to him," Rock said.

"I didn't do anything to you. I just blocked the jerk's alpha powers from reaching you."

"You can do that?" Hannah asked, surprised.

"Apparently. I've never tried before."

Rock shook his head at Cede. "I am not going to ask her that...No, you can't transform here...Fine. Cede wants to know if you can do that permanently to his head."

Cede pushed his head up into her hand and flashed his blue pleading puppy-dog eyes at her. She laughed and rubbed his head. "Sorry. I don't think that would be a good idea. You need to be able to communicate with the rest of the pack and my shield probably blocks telepathy too."

Cede whined.

"He wants to know if you could make the shield so it just works on alpha powers."

"Maybe. I don't know. I just learned how to do them. I can do some research. Is there a problem with your new alpha?"

"He says Alpha Aki is fine," Rock said. "It's the other alphas he has an issue with. They force people to do things they shouldn't." Rock frowned at Cede. "What are you talking about? What were you forced to do? That's...I'm sorry."

"What did he say?" Honey asked.

Rock shook his head angrily. "He was...abused. It's no wonder he ran away."

The outrage in Rock's scent suggested it was more than just beatings, but Honey didn't press. She knelt down and put her arms around Cede's neck. His fur was soft against her bare arms and neck. Cede pressed his head against hers. It seemed like years since she'd had a good wolf hug. "I'll see if I can make you a charm or something. I wouldn't want to permanently do something to your head."

His head turned and her neck was suddenly wetter than her sweat had made it. She pushed him away and rubbed at the spot with her shirt. "You had to go and ruin a perfectly good hug, didn't you."

From the way he was sitting there with his tongue hanging out, like he was laughing again, he wasn't sorry at all.

"All right, lover boy, that's enough. We need to finish our rounds and get back. I've got to train," Rock said.

"Train for what?" Honey asked while she stood to wipe off her knees.

He flexed a muscle. "Pack trials. There's a mid-summer competition between the packs. The top ten from each pack compete in ten events and get points when they win. The pack with the most points at the end is declared the champion."

"What are the events?"

"Oh, you know, running, jumping, javelin throwing, normal track stuff."

"MMA?"

"That too."

"That sounds like fun." Did the packs back home do the same thing? It sounded like something they'd do. She could ask her friends in four days. Four days! "Are you and Cede competing too," she asked Hannah.

Hannah gave Honey a disgruntled look.

"Hannah is, although she thinks such competitions are barbaric." Rock responded. "Alpha Aki encourages everyone to try, but maybe not Cede. He cheats."

Cede barked.

"He says he wasn't cheating, he just didn't realize there were rules."

"Right," Hannah scoffed.

"I wish I could compete," Honey sighed. "The other witches are great, but I only know of one of them who runs, and she's always busy."

"I could ask Alpha Aki if you could come watch," Rock offered generously. Hannah looked at him like he'd sprouted another head.

"Oh, that would be..." stupid. Her protections had worked so far, but it would be both irresponsible and dangerous to expose herself to an entire pack where she couldn't freeze her way out. Not to mention, Ms. Charming would have a heart attack. "I can't," she sighed.

"Yeah, he'd probably say no anyway."

"Where is it and when?" Maybe she could jog by.

"Next weekend at the sports park. It's south of the river past Meadowlily road if you keep going the way you are."

"In the mean pack's territory?"

"Yeah. That's another reason Cede isn't going to compete. No point in stirring up a hornet's nest, eh."

"Were they the ones you ran from?" Honey asked.

Cede shook his head.

"He had a couple of run-ins with them when he was rogue," Rock explained.

"Oh. Sorry to hear that."

Cede pushed his head into her hand again and she gave him another rub. His eagerness reminded her of Luca which sent a pang of longing through her so strongly that she found herself fighting not to cry. "I better go."

16

MEETING IN SECRET

"Isabelle, I am so glad you are here. I know you usually work weekends, but Darling called in sick again and we need another person on the floor. Can you stay a few hours?"

Misty, the manager, looked frazzled. Her normally neat ponytail was askew, and her T-shirt was almost untucked. It *was* oddly busy at the climbing center for a Thursday evening.

Honey unclipped her harness from the safety rope and stepped away from the wall to let the next person on. She'd only come in to climb the walls because it felt like she was literally climbing the walls back at the school while waiting until it was time to go to the library to contact the guys.

"Any other night and I would, but not tonight. I have something I have to do. I'm sorry."

"No, no, I understand." Misty was already looking around for her next victim.

"Rosemary just left," Honey said helpfully. "I'm sure she would like the hours."

"Good idea." Like magic, the manager's phone appeared in her hand, or maybe it had never left.

Honey glanced at her watch. An hour-and-a-half to go. Plenty of time to get back to the school, shower, then walk to the library and claim a computer.

It was pouring outside. By the time she got to school, she felt like she'd jumped in a lake or two or three. Unfortunately, Ms. Charming did not appear to dry her off when she stepped inside. The other, drier, students hurried to get out of her way while she sloshed up to the third floor and directly into the shower to warm up.

Her shoes were soaked. Good thing she'd finally bought a second pair. Cleaner and drier, she grabbed her backpack and jogged down the stairs. It was still early enough that she could grab something to eat.

"Isabelle, did you leave the puddles all over the entrance hall?"

"Sorry Ms. Charming. I got caught in the rain."

"Well go mop them up. I'm not your mother."

"Yes, Ma'am."

She was grumpy.

"And where are you going? Are you going out again? Why do you have your backpack?"

"I'm going to the library. I have some things to look up."

"To the college!?"

"No. The one just down the street."

"What are you looking up?"

"Scholarships, colleges, things like that."

"You're not visiting any web sites you shouldn't, are you? I've heard stories."

"No, Ma'am. I can show you my notes."

Ms. Charming shook her head. "I really don't know what your aunt was thinking, letting you go to college at your age."

Why did people always think she couldn't handle college? "By the way, I'm just about through the second-year text on spell-crafting. Miss Evelstone said to ask you if you had a copy of Advanced Spell-crafting I could borrow."

"Through the second book already are you? Let's see how well you are retaining the knowledge. Shields up."

Honey did as she commanded. The air between them was suddenly covered in a rainbow of colors.

"And now you can't see."

Honey made the outer layer of her shield fall to the floor while at the same time adding another layer to the back.

"Hmm. Decent, but now you have another mess to clean up."

Ms. Charming was being mean. That wasn't like her at all. "Is something wrong Ms. Charming?"

"No. Long, dreary day." She sighed and waved her hand at the puddle of color. "I guess that was actually my mess. Oh, Mrs. Wixx sent you something. She said her seer friend said you'd need it." She pulled a small envelope out of her pocket.

"Thank you," Honey said, taking it eagerly. She'd rarely received any letters in her life. It felt like there was a coin inside.

"I wish mail still made me that excited. That's what happens I guess when all you get are bills."

"Is the school in trouble?" Honey asked, looking up from the mystery note.

"No, the school is fine. One of the girls decided a washing machine that spewed soap all over the basement would be funny. It was like a soapy winter wonderland down there. Luckily, I was able to reverse it."

"What if you put a charm on it that did something, like growl or spray water at them when people tried to spell the machines?"

"That would just make some girls try much harder to spell them." She paused, then chuckled. "Maybe I should. It would keep them from getting into mischief elsewhere."

"Please leave the fourth one alone."

"That one already has a protective spell on it. The other teachers threatened to quit if I didn't have one working machine. I, of course, don't need to wash my clothes."

"I'm surprised you don't sell charms to clean clothes."

"Who says I don't?"

Ms. Charming pranced off to her office, looking a little less stormy than before. Honey pulled the mop out of the closet, made short work of the water, then headed for the dining room. She'd missed the official dinner, but there were always snacks available. She grabbed a few bars and an orange, then headed back out into the rain, this time with one of the school umbrellas.

The library was quieter than usual, perhaps because of the rain. She claimed a computer in the back corner where no one could read over her shoulder and signed into the chat room a good fifteen minutes before 8 pm. Knowing she was just minutes away from hearing from her friends, it was hard to sit still. Her heart thrummed excitedly in her chest.

She needed a distraction. Her grandmother's letter would do nicely.

The lump in the letter turned out to be a nickel that was sealed in a cute little zip-lock bag. She pulled out the letter that came with it, put the coin back inside the envelope, and unfolded the note.

Dear Isabelle,

I hear you're adjusting well and leaning at impressive speeds. I'm sure your aunt would be proud of you. I would if you were my niece.

My seer friend had another vision of you. She said you'd need this in Boston. She refused to tell me why you would go to Boston or when, of course. She said it would be good for you to go, so I guess I can't tell you not to go. It's a charm if you haven't already figured that out. It will change your appearance for up to 6 hours but no more. You can turn it on and off in that time if you need to. All you have to do is hold it in your hand for twenty seconds. It's supposed to be good enough to trick a magic detector, although I'm not encouraging you to test that.

Stay safe and good luck,
Love, R.W.

Boston. She had been thinking about it ever since she'd learned that the grimoire of the man who'd cursed the land Zavier was hoping to obtain for his pack might be locked up there. She'd looked in every book she could think of in the library for more information on Mr. Witthem and his curse. She'd even asked the librarian for a book via the interlibrary loan system, but it wasn't helpful.

If she could get a look at the grimoire, maybe it would tell her how to break the curse.

With a quick search in an incognito window, she discovered it would take over 9 hours to drive to Boston and 24 hours by bus and train. By plane, though, was an hour and thirty minutes and less than $300 round trip. The biggest problem in getting to Boston was that Ms. Charming would never agree to let her go. The second biggest was keeping her new name and picture from being associated with a flight to Boston or Boston at all. She could easily don a disguise once she got past the gate in the airport. It wouldn't have to be the one her grandma had sent, just one to hide her from the cameras everywhere. However, her new name and picture would still be in a database somewhere. She wanted to avoid that. Too bad shooting magic at cameras to blur her image didn't work. All she'd managed to do was crash the internet connection at the library by trying it on the computers there, much to the irritation of her fellow patrons.

It was cliché but maybe she could pretend to go on a sleepover somewhere like they did in movies. She'd have to have someone back up her story, Frederica perhaps, but Frederica would want to go with her. Was it possible to get a flight to Boston and back in one day? That way she wouldn't have to find or pay for a hotel and when she got back, she could stay with Frederica.

One minute to go. She could look for flights later.

The wait was agonizing. A minute passed, two, five, ten. Her eager anticipation started to fade into disappointment. Thirty minutes later, she told herself they weren't going to show, but she couldn't pull away. She searched every line that popped up for Luca's creative names or the code word, pizza, hoping and praying. Had she been wrong about the time zone? She should be on the same one as them. Had they decided it was safer to stay away from her? No. They wouldn't do that. Her messages probably got lost in the mail. She'd just have to try again with a different remailer service. Maybe she'd send them to Luca and Liam this time.

The library closed at 9. She stayed in her seat until the librarian came by and asked her to finish up.

Her friends never showed.

17

SICK DAY

"Isabelle, are you okay?"

"What?" Honey rolled over and blinked at the bright light. It was morning already?

Miss Evelstone sat on the edge of Honey's bed. "You didn't show up for class this morning. I was worried."

"What time is it?"

"Ten already."

"Oh. Oh! I'm sorry. I'll get up. I must have forgot to set my alarm."

"Is something going on?"

Could Miss Evelstone tell she'd cried herself to sleep? Her nose did feel stuffy.

"No." Not anything she could talk about.

"Are you feeling okay?" Miss Evelstone put the back of her hand against Honey's forehead. "You feel hot."

"I run warm."

"You sound stuffy too. Does your throat hurt?"

Now that she mentioned it, "A little, but I'm sure it's nothing. I just need a drink."

Miss Evelstone gave her a 'we both know better' look. "I think you've been pushing yourself too hard. Take a

135

break today. Sleep or read something fun, or better, go to the movies and just don't think for a while. If that sore throat doesn't go away, go see the school healer, okay? I'll need you bright and smiling Monday morning to greet our new set of campers."

"Okay."

Miss Evelstone pushed a messy strand of curls away from Honey's cheek. "You know you can talk to me if something is going on, right? I was sixteen once too, and not that long ago."

If only she could. "That's really nice of you."

Miss Evelstone shrugged. "You're a good helper. It's hard to find good help."

"Thanks."

Miss Evelstone chuckled and patted Honey's shoulder. "See you Monday. I'll tell Ms. Charming I gave you the day off."

She didn't want a day off. She wanted to hear from her friends.

They were okay. They had to be. She hadn't seen anything in the Indiana headlines, although it would have to be really bad to show up in the human news. Did the witches have a news service? They must have. She did remember seeing some papers in the college library.

She stayed under the covers another quarter hour before finally rolling out of bed. Maybe she *was* sick. Her head pounded like someone had stuffed a pillow in it. She hadn't felt so ill in years, not since – she couldn't remember. Had she ever been sick?

She shouldn't be sick. She was half wolf. Ah…maybe that was the problem. She hadn't transformed since, well, since she was kidnapped over a month ago. Although it wasn't really that long ago, it felt like years.

She grabbed the shower caddy someone had left behind at the end of the term and plodded down the hall to the bathroom. Not another soul was around. Most of the campers were housed downstairs and they were all currently in class. Transforming inside a school of witches was dangerous, extremely so, but she didn't know where else to go except maybe to the bathroom at work. With her head feeling like it did, getting dressed was more than she wanted to do. She needed relief now and the only place with any privacy was the bathroom.

The bathroom had four stalls for toilets and four for showers with no lock on the main door. She dragged the small bench students set their supplies on while they were showering in front of the door to give herself some warning in case someone walked in, then turned on the water. Not wanting to stand next to a toilet in wolf form, she stepped into the shower and transformed under the spray. A good five minutes passed with the warm water massaging her head and the steam filling her nose. No one came in. No alarms went off that she could hear. She transformed back into human form and finished her shower, already feeling better.

Now, what to do with herself? She didn't want to watch a movie, not alone.

Well, if she was going to Boston, she needed to do some research. She snagged some food from the kitchen and, instead of jogging, took a bus to the campus library.

The librarian of the magical college library in London always acted happy to see her, unlike Ms. Carrier, the magical librarian at the college in Indiana. The Canadian librarian didn't sneak up on people either. She was what Honey had always imagined a grandmother would be until she'd met her own. The older lady smiled when she saw Honey approaching and even remembered her fake name.

"Good afternoon, Isabelle. What can I help you with today?"

"Do you have any books on the library system?"

"On the library system?"

"Yes, I was curious about the history. How long has it been around? When was the first magical library established, things like that."

The white-haired witch put her palm to her chest as if she'd never been more flattered. "It's not very often I get a request for information on the library. There is, in fact a very nice book on the subject, written by, get this, a librarian!"

"No!"

"Unbelievable, eh?" the woman grinned. "Just a moment, I'll see if it's available."

She opened a notebook and moved her finger across it like she was writing. Words appeared at the bottom of the page, too small for Honey to read over the desk and upside-down.

"There's a copy in Toronto that's available. I sent in a request."

"Just now?"

"I bet you thought touchscreens were a new invention. Nope. Witches have been using them to send messages for ages. The humans finally caught up with us."

"Why do witches use regular phones and computers then?" Honey asked.

"I'm guessing you didn't grow up in a covenstead, eh?"

"No."

"Well, witches who live in a wiccan community tend to use witch tech more than witches who live around humans, for hopefully obvious reasons."

"Magical interference and to keep the humans oblivious," Honey summed.

"Yes."

The notebook beeped. The woman glanced at the page again. "Ah, it's ready already. Have you ever seen a book portal? No? I'll leave the door open so you can watch."

The librarian opened the door behind the desk and propped it opened with a rubber door stop. On the back wall in the next room, Honey saw three square cabinet doors about two feet across. A circle of light glowed above the middle one. The librarian picked up a cone-looking object hanging next to the middle door and spoke, "That you, Gladys?"

"No, it's Percy. I have your request."

"Thank you, Percy. Opening the door now."

She put the cone back and lifted the latch holding the door shut. Behind the door, the surface of the wall looked different, like it was a fluid instead of a solid. A corner of a book abruptly marred the smooth surface. The librarian grabbed the corner and a moment later, had the whole book in her hands.

"I got it. Thank you, Percy," she said into the cone, then shut the cabinet door and latched it again.

"Are the portals always on?" Honey asked.

"Yes, of course, unless they're broken. They're expensive and need to be maintained at least once a year but are cheaper and faster than using a mailing service."

"Do they always go to the same place?"

"Have you never used a portal before?"

"No."

"Well, I have a very nice book on portals too, if you'd like to take a look."

"I would, but later. Can you tell me the basics?"

"For sure. Yes, they stay in one place."

"Are your portals only for non-animate objects or can living things pass through too?"

"I don't think portals care what or who passes through them, they just can't be doing magic at the time."

"What if someone is wearing or using a charm?"

"Shouldn't be a problem as long as they don't activate the charm inside the portal."

"How far can portals go?"

"Thousands of miles, but the shorter they are, the more stable they are."

"So, if I wanted a book from…" better pick something other than Boston, "Florida, do you have to make a new portal or can you program these to go other places?"

"These are the only three portals in this library. Every library is connected to at least three. If you want a book from a library not connected to this library, then you have to use multiple portals. Generally, the maximum number a book has to pass through is five, but most don't have to go that far. From Florida, for example, a book would pass through Alabama, Indiana, and Toronto before it got to here."

"Indiana?"

"Yes. Indiana is a major hub and so is Toronto. All the major hubs are connected. Toronto is the one closest to us."

"Indiana? As in the…" her lips abruptly couldn't form the word 'library'. Honey quickly adjusted her sentence. "You mean Vindale U?"

"Yes. Have you been there?"

"Mmm," Honey replied noncommittally. "If a person wanted to portal from Florida to here, would they have to use multiple portals too?"

"Maybe. There are a few permanent portals in the major cities, but usually witches just use a temporary one to get directly where they are going without fuss. Well, except for the side effects. Portal travel is not for the faint of stomach."

"You know what, I'd like to look at the portal book too."

The woman grinned like she'd just made a big sale. "Coming right up."

"Also, where would I buy a notebook like that?" Honey asked, pointing to the librarian's notebook.

The librarian's grin widened even farther and she flipped a business card out of her pocket. "I happen to know a lovely girl who makes something like them."

"And you carry her business card around in your pocket?" Honey asked skeptically.

"Only when she is my granddaughter."

The book on libraries included a rough map of the National Council Library in Boston and all the collections stored there including the 'Forbidden' books. Honey guessed that was where Mr. Witthem's grimoire would be. The book also gave instructions on how to request access to books in the collections. Could it be that easy? Would they let her look at it if she just asked? The author then went on to describe a few of the magical alarms and deadly defensive spells put into place. He was very clear that it was only a sampling of what was there. If what he said was true, there was no way she'd be able to break in to read the grimoire. She'd have to ask permission.

On the plus side, she'd found a way to get to Boston quickly and without being tracked. All she needed to do was find a portal maker who wouldn't tell anyone where she'd gone. She'd also found a potentially untraceable way to communicate with her friends, one that did not require a portal or going undercover. She just had to figure out how to send a magic notebook to her friends.

18

MAGIC SLATES

The address on the business card the librarian had handed her was a few blocks from the public library and belonged to a brick building that in a former life had probably been a warehouse. It had two floors of shops, mostly carrying witchcraft-associated products, and the center of the building was open so that buyers could see all the first-floor shops from the second floor. Honey was pretty sure some of the customers were human.

She followed the numbers above the shops to the very back corner of the first floor. The shop was so small there was just enough room for Honey to step in and stand in front of the chunky desk jammed across the middle of it. The instant Honey's shadow touched the desk, the gum-smacking, pony-tailed girl behind the desk put down her romance novel and pulled up a bright grin. The girl's grin looked a lot like her grandmother's.

"Hello. Can I help you?"

"I hope so. I was talking with your grandmother in the library and she had this notebook that she could write in and send messages. She said you sell them."

The girl straightened and nodded professionally. "Well, not exactly like hers. Those notebooks are complicated. They come with a lot of other features and they're not cheap. If you just want to text though, you've come to the right place."

"I do."

She pulled something out of the desk drawer and plunked it on the desk. "This is what you want then."

On the desk were two pieces of cardboard about the size of her hand each with a happy face drawn above gray squares. A small plastic stylus was in a simple holder above the gray square.

Honey's hope fizzled.

"What is it?" she asked.

"It's called a Magic Slate. It was popular with humans in the last century, but you can still buy them, obviously." The girl pulled one of the styluses out and drew on one of the gray squares. "See, you write your message and it appears on both the first slate and the one that is paired to it. When either you or the receiver lifts the plastic," she lifted the part she'd just wrote on, "it disappears off both slates."

"Do you have anything less conspicuous?"

"You think this is conspicuous?"

"Well, if I saw someone using it, I'd wonder what it was."

"You think moving your finger over a plain piece of paper or a notebook would be less noticeable?" the girl challenged.

"Yes."

"No it wouldn't. This is perfect for passing messages. It's small enough to fit in your pocket and sturdy enough not to bend. Plus, it's easier to draw with a stylus than your finger. You can cut off the happy face if you want. I just thought they were fun."

"Can the messages be traced?" Honey asked.

"Well, sure, if you push too hard and mark up the wax underneath."

"No, I mean, could someone bug the slate like you can bug a computer and listen in or track where they are coming from?"

"Why would someone do that?"

"Just wondering if it was possible."

"Sure, if they had the resources. Magic can do just about anything, but most people don't have portal magic."

"This is portal magic?"

"Yeah. That's how the messages are sent. Ever heard of the Felix family."

"Yes. Are you part of the Felix family?"

"Distant cousin, but yes."

"Do you know Frederica? She's a friend of mine. I thought she was going to go to summer camp at the school, but I haven't heard from her."

"Oh, you wouldn't have."

"Why?"

"Her magic came in and she accidentally portalled herself somewhere. She's been missing for days."

She said it calmly, like that was normal. Was it for witches?

"Is it hard to portal back to a specific location?"

"It shouldn't be. The more familiar you are with a place, the easier it is to portal to, or so I've been told. I'm not powerful enough to make a human-sized portal on my own. It's more likely she's lost somewhere in the in-between."

"The in-between?"

"Yeah."

"Can she get un-lost?"

The girl shrugged. "I don't know. I've never heard of it happening. Her poor sister is still freaking out. She was there when it happened. She said she tried to stop Frederica from stepping through, but Frederica was so excited about her powers, she did it anyway."

"Are you talking about Victoria?" Honey asked.

"Yes. Do you know her too?"

The girl clearly didn't have a clue how evil Victoria was. If Victoria was involved, Honey was pretty sure Frederica had not disappeared into a portal, but was trapped, thanks again to her sister.

"Yes. I might be able to find Frederica. Is there a way I can see where she disappeared?"

"Do you make portals too?"

"No. I can detect spells. Maybe I can tell what went wrong."

"Oh. Okay. Let me write my uncle."

The girl pulled out another slate, this one with a unicorn on top. A minute later, the wall at the back of the little shop rippled and a skinny man with thinning, wispy hair stepped out.

"That was fast," the girl said.

"My wife was about to write to someone. What's this about someone finding Frederica?"

Honey stuck out her hand. "Hi, I'm Isabelle. I'm Frederica's friend. I don't know if she told you this, but she disappeared for a day at school. I was able to find her because I can sense spells. I thought maybe I could help this time."

"No, I didn't know. She never said anything."

Why hadn't Frederica told her parents what Victoria had done? Was she afraid of what Victoria would do to her?

"You should ask her if I find her."

"Oh, I will. Follow me. We'll portal directly to my house."

"Hey, do you want these?" the girl asked, holding up the slates.

"How much?"

"Fifty for the two of them."

"Fifty?" Honey had no idea if that was fair or not. It seemed like a lot. "How long do these last?"

"A year, at least," the girl said, "then you have to bring them back and I'll recharge them."

"For free?"

"No."

"I'll give you ten." Honey said.

"Ten each," the girl countered.

She probably didn't sell much sitting in the back corner where she was. "Here." Honey handed the girl a twenty and took the smiling slates. "It's worth it if they work."

"Thank you, and have a nice day," the girl grinned.

The librarian was right. Portal travel was not for the weak of stomach. The moment Honey stepped through the portal that Frederica's dad made in the wall, all her molecules abruptly accelerated forward so fast, it felt like a part of her was left behind, then just as suddenly, they snapped back inside of her. She had to swallow several times to keep from losing the contents of her stomach on the sunny, enclosed porch where she now stood.

"First time?" the man asked.

Honey nodded, afraid to open her mouth. After about ten seconds though, she was able to take a deep breath and smile.

"Better?"

Honey nodded.

"She disappeared in the dining room," the man said, stepping around a metal rocking couch and toward the door into the house. Honey followed him.

Inside was bright and colorful. The kitchen on her right had light teal-colored cabinets, wooden counters, and pale yellow walls that were abruptly cut off by burnt orange walls that extended to Honey's left. She guessed that was the dining room, since there was a large white table and matching chairs with yellow seat cushions.

"Anything?" the man asked.

"No, but she probably moved. Will you show me all the spots she likes to hang out in?"

"This is where she disappeared."

"If it's a spell, it's on her, not the room."

He nodded. "This way then."

He led her past a U-shaped sectional in front of a large TV, then down a long hallway to a pale green door. "This is her room."

Honey knocked before she opened it to be polite. "Frederica, if you're in there, it's Isabelle."

There was movement behind her at the same moment she opened the door. She didn't have a chance to see what was behind her because she was suddenly engulfed by a pair of arms attached to a body that hadn't seen a shower for a few days.

"Isabelle, thank goodness. You can see me, right?"

"Yes."

"What is it," the man beside her demanded. "What do you sense?"

Honey grabbed a handful of the invisible spell that coated Frederica and as the girl stepped back, Honey tugged it off. "I found her."

"Frederica!"

"Dad!"

Honey stepped out of the way and nearly ran into Victoria who was watching a few feet away. She didn't look mad, but she didn't look happy either.

"We need to talk," Honey told her.

Victoria gave a nod and led her back down the hallway, past a woman who came running from somewhere else in the house, to the porch outside.

"Could you see her this whole time?" Honey asked as soon as Victoria shut the door.

"Yes."

"Why do you keep spelling your sister?"

"How did you remove the spell," the girl countered.

"I just pulled it off."

Victoria turned her back on Honey. "I don't mean to spell her. She is just so...so irritating sometimes." She looked back over her shoulder. "Surely, you've noticed how much she talks. She never shuts up."

Honey shrugged. "She has a lot to say." It was odd a fire witch could turn people invisible, plus, Victoria smelled like wool, not asphalt. Oh. "You're not really a fire witch, are you?"

Victoria turned her head to look back out over the porch railing without answering.

Honey stepped to the rail beside her. "I'm not going to tell anyone. I just think your ability to turn people invisible is better. I mean, how many witches can do that?"

"Criminal ones."

"I bet other people would find invisibility useful too. You could probably make a lot of money selling charms to the Enforcers if you can learn to package it and how to remove it."

Victoria shook her head, knocking loose a tear in the process. "That's just it, I can't remove it. I tried. The spell was like a curse. Not only did I make it impossible to see her, I made it impossible for anyone to hear her or for her to even communicate. I saw her try and move things to get mom's attention, but she couldn't."

"You're probably just overdoing the spell a little. Maybe I can help. I can see spells. Make the couch invisible and I'll walk you through how to remove the spell."

"Why would you help me? You're Frederica's friend."

"Yeah, and I don't want her to get stuck invisible for days again."

The door slammed open behind them. The woman they'd passed in the hall stormed out onto the porch with Frederica and her dad following meekly behind. "Victoria Wendy Felix, you have some explaining to do."

Honey was between the woman and Victoria, clearly not a safe place to be. She slipped out of the woman's line of sight toward the screen door that led off the porch. "I'll just wait outside."

19

UNBOUND

The Felixes lived in a covenstead. It wasn't in the middle of a field like her grandma's was, but all the surrounding houses were obviously witch houses. The one next door had a garden full of herbs that were lusher than she'd ever seen and the one across the street had paint that changed color every few minutes. Interestingly, the few neighbors she saw didn't pay any attention at all to the yelling now coming from the Felix's back yard. Were they being polite or could they not hear it? Maybe the Felixes had a spell to prevent their neighbors from hearing.

"Sorry about that," Frederica said, coming around the house several minutes later. "She had it coming."

"She's jealous of you, you know."

"I know. I don't know what to do about it though."

"Maybe it will be better now that she knows what her power is."

"Maybe, if mom ever lets her use it," Frederica snickered.

"How can she stop her?"

"Inhibitor. When we really do something wrong, mom magics it on us and grounds us at the same time, well, she

152

just grounds me since my magic still hasn't come in." She gave a huge sigh.

"Is that normal for someone with your skills? I thought all witches started getting magic when they are young." She hadn't ever asked anyone, but Honey had been able to see molecules as long as she could remember.

"I did have a little magic for a while, then it went away. Mom says the same thing happened to her when she was young. She says it's safer this way. I will have 'a strong theoretical foundation and the maturity to make good decisions when it finally comes in'," Frederica mimicked. "She doesn't realize or care that I won't know how to make a portal because I never got to practice."

"Did your dad's powers come in late too?"

"No. Everyone else got their power when they were ten. Mine is nearly five years late."

"It's really odd. I can sense your magic. I don't think I would sense it if you didn't have it. Are you wearing an inhibitor or any jewelry?"

"No."

Honey switched to her other sight. "Turn around, slowly."

Honey couldn't see anything, but when she took a deep breath, she could smell rope.

"Can I stop now?"

"No. Keep going."

There. It was just a sparkle, but there was another one. She put her finger over the sparkle on Frederica's arm, effectively stopping her from spinning. Honey could almost feel something tiny, like thread, beneath her fingertip. She traced it around Frederica's arm to her back.

"What are you doing?"

"Lift up your hair."

A tiny bow made from shimmering string was tied at the base of Frederica's neck, at least that's what Honey imagined the spell looked like. Honey grabbed one end of the string and pulled. The bow fell apart easily. Like a silk ribbon, the thin, magical filaments wrapped around Frederica's body slipped away and fluttered to the ground where they disappeared.

"Oh." Frederica said. She held up her hands and a wavering sphere appeared above them. "I have magic." She dropped her hands and flung her arms around Honey's neck and started jumping up and down. "I have magic! I have magic! I have magic! Dad!"

Honey could suddenly breath again as Frederica released her and sprinted to the man just coming around the house. "My magic is here!"

"Really?"

"Yes. Look."

She made the sphere thing again.

Frederica's dad put his arm around her shoulders and squeezed her tightly. "That's great honey."

"What's great?" Frederica's mom asked, coming around the same corner her husband had.

"Frederica's magic just came in."

Instead of grinning like a maniac like Frederica and her dad were doing, Frederica's mom's face went stormy. She pressed her lips together and breathed through her nose like a mad bull.

"No. You put those powers away. You are forbidden to use them. No daughter of mine is going to become a teen mother."

Frederica stopped grinning to frown at her mother. "What are you talking about?"

"I have seen it. You, with a little baby in your arms and some brown-haired boy named Luca. Who names a boy Luca?"

"Mom, I don't even know any boys."

"For a reason! No boys until you're twenty."

"Dear, are you sure the baby was hers," her husband asked carefully.

"That Luca was looking at our daughter like she was his sun."

"Really?" Frederica asked eagerly.

"What does the boy have to do with Frederica's powers?" Frederica's father asked.

"She portalled there. If she hadn't portalled there she never would have met him."

No longer smiling, Mr. Felix looked down at Frederica. "Did your powers come in by themselves or did you do something?"

Frederica grinned over at Honey. Honey shook her head and widened her eyes, willing her not to say anything, but Frederica didn't get the message. "Isabelle did something. Tell them Isabelle."

Honey braced herself. "There was a spell wrapped around her. I untied it."

"You did what?!" Frederica's mother screeched. "Do you know how much I paid for that? You don't go around undoing spells without asking young lady. Didn't your mother teach you anything? Where is it? You put that back on her right now."

Honey wasn't sure whether to back away from the approaching storm or freeze her. Frederica's dad stepped in front of the woman before Honey could decide.

"Felicity, what are you talking about? What spell?"

"I bound her. I bound her powers to protect her so she'd never meet that boy."

"You bound our daughter's powers, our beautiful daughter who's only ever wanted to do magic with her family, for five years because of a vision which wasn't even bad?" His voice had gone all soft, but there was an undercurrent of danger that made Honey wish she was anywhere else.

Frederica's mom poked her husband's chest. "You want our daughter to be a teenage mother?"

"I want her to be happy. You have not made her happy. It's one thing to bind our daughters' powers for a week, which I'm not sure I agree with, but for five years when she didn't do anything wrong?"

"She will."

"You don't know that!" Frederica's father roared.

"Edward, shh. The neighbors will hear."

"Our neighbors have long since invested in good earplugs or are currently enjoying a nice cup of tea as they gaze at the spectacle you have made of our family in the front yard!" He waved to a neighboring house. The man standing in the window waved back, then took a sip out of his steaming mug.

Frederica's dad turned his back on his wife. "Isabelle, Frederica, you're with me." He flipped his finger in a circle

156

toward the broad tree in his front yard and stomped toward it. Honey kept her eyes averted from Frederica's mom and obediently followed him. A few moments later, she stepped out of the tree behind Frederica and into the entrance hall of the school.

Frederica's dad took a deep breath that might have been a sigh, then turned with a smile toward Honey. "Sorry about that. Isabelle, right?"

Honey shrugged. "It's okay. These things happen."

"Still, you not only rescued Frederica, you unbound her powers. I should have realized…" he shook his head. "Here." He thrust his fist at her then flipped his hand over and uncurled his fingers. Two little brown nuts sat in his palm.

"Acorns?"

He chuckled. "Not just acorns, portacorns or pocorns or portanuts. I'm still deciding on a name."

"Daa-ad," Frederica moaned.

"They have something to do with portals?" Honey guessed.

"They're charms. You hold one in your palm in front of a door or wall, anything solid, and picture where you want to go. It should be another wall or door that you know exists without anything in front of them. You do not want to step through a wall and into a toilet. Trust me. If your vision is clear enough, the charm will activate and you can step through. Each acorn has enough power for one portal, which is why I'm giving you two. Round trip portals."

Honey carefully took them from his hand. "Wow. Thank you. How far can I travel with one of these?"

"As far as you want, as long as it's on the surface of the Earth. I added safeguards so people can't portal into a volcano or an ocean or anything dangerous."

"Smart."

"I have to be with the idiots out there."

"Anything else I should know?"

"They expire in a year and you can let more than one person use them but they only last for ten seconds or until the caster goes through it."

"This is just what I needed," Honey said sincerely. "Thank you."

"You are very welcome." He turned to his daughter. "Okay Frederica, are you ready to make your first-ever portal?"

"You bet I am!"

It seemed like a big thing to try right after getting her powers, but what did she know? Honey stepped back while Frederica swirled her finger just like her father had at the wall. The wall rippled. Frederica's father took his daughter's hand and smiled down at her.

"Where are we going?"

"Vancouver Island."

"Good choice."

Before Honey could say goodbye, they were gone.

Back in her room at school Honey contemplated her portacorns. Where should she go? What if she popped into one of the boys' houses? They'd be so surprised. Maybe they could watch a movie or play games or have a slumber party. She let herself imagine their hugs and what each boy would say. In the end though, after she'd wiped away more than a few tears, she put away the idea. It was too risky. The boys would understand that she couldn't stay, but their families wouldn't. For the same reason, she couldn't drop in on Luna Lynn either, although if she did, maybe she could get her bike. Yeah, a motorcycle would go over well with Ms. Charming, not.

Another option was to portal to Boston, but after reading the book, she was positive the witches would have protections around the library to prevent people from portalling in, not to mention she'd never been there and wouldn't know a safe place to make a portal.

What if she used her portacorn to go to the library at Vindale? She could portal from there into Boston through the Vindale library's portal, assuming she could still get into the Vindale library. As a bonus, even if she couldn't get to Boston through the library portal, she could leave the magic slate for the boys in the library or on campus, then she wouldn't have to worry about anyone intercepting it in the mail and putting a tracing spell on it.

There were only two problems with that plan. First, she wasn't sure where the portals were in the Vindale library, and second, she'd have to unlock the door blocking the portal in Boston, assuming there was one, from inside the portal. She couldn't do magic inside the portal, so she couldn't transform and simply make the door disappear under her hands.

What if she made a charm to do the same thing? If she tossed the charm through the portal and made it activate only after it hit the door, she would avoid doing magic in the portal itself.

Getting the charm right could take a while, but she didn't have to go tonight.

Someone knocked on the door.

She quickly stuffed the portacorns in her pocket and crossed the room to open the door. "Miss Evelstone?"

"Hey. Just thought I'd check on you. How are you feeling?"

"Better."

Miss Evelstone eyed Honey's cheek. Had she missed a tear? She quickly rubbed her cheek in what she hoped looked like a completely normal motion.

"You sure?"

"Yeah."

"Are you coming tonight?"

"Tonight?"

"Full moon, remember?"

"Oh, um no, I hadn't." On second thought, going to the Boston tonight might be a great idea. All the witches would be occupied with coven meetings. She just had to figure out how to make that charm. "Do you think it would be all right if I stayed here? I thought I would turn in early."

"Sure. I'll tell Ms. Charming, and remember, if you need to talk about anything or anyone, boys for example, I'm here."

"Thank you."

If only it was something as simple as boys, Honey thought as Miss Evelstone shut the door.

20

FROZEN

This was stupid. There was no need to expose herself to a bunch of wolves. Sure, if she didn't know they were gathering in the park and happened to run past, it shouldn't matter. Even if they realized she was a witch due to her lack of smell it shouldn't matter.

She did know though.

Seriously, she should be running in the opposite direction. She still could. All she had to do was turn around.

"Isabelle!"

Her heart jumped. She squinted at the gangly figure sprinting her way and prepared to freeze him, then relaxed.

"Cede. What are you doing here? I thought you would be at the park."

"Warm-up jog," Cede panted when he reached her and turned to run by her side back toward the two other guys jogging their way. One was Rock, but she didn't recognize the other.

"They're going to let you participate?" Honey asked.

161

"Only against people from our own pack," Rock responded before Cede could. He stopped and waited for Honey and Cede to reach them.

"The events haven't started yet?" she asked. She'd timed her run so she'd pass by around 8 am, early enough that she'd have time to take a shower at work before her shift began at 9, but hopefully after the events had started so the wolves would be less likely to notice her.

"They have," Rock replied, "but Cede here was bouncing all over the place like an excited little puppy. Alpha Aki asked me to take him for a run before he got into trouble. Think you could, you know." He nodded at Cede's head.

She looked up and down the long, barely two-lane, tree-lined road. The only people she saw were behind them and heading in the opposite direction.

"Sure."

She barely had her hands lifted before Cede was pushing his head eagerly into her fingers. She massaged his scalp a little, the way he seemed to like in his wolf form, then closed her eyes and dove into his brain. There were a few sluggish blobs, or maybe they were the normal ones and Cede's other brain molecules spun faster when he was excited. They all seemed very fast.

"Is he okay?" Rock asked when she removed her fingers.

Cede gave a little whine, then suddenly threw his arms around her and laid his head on her shoulder. She stumbled under his weight, then put her arms around him in return.

"Cede!" Rock admonished.

"It's okay." She put her head against Cede's and squeezed. She was all wet with sweat, but if he didn't care, she wasn't going to push him away. She hadn't had a good hug in a while and she bet Cede hadn't either, not as a human anyway.

"I think so, although his molecules do seem very active. Can I look in your head for a comparison?"

"Why? Do you think there's something wrong?"

"No. It's probably normal, but I haven't looked into heads when people were excited about something. I assume you're excited about today too, though, right?"

"Not like Cede, but I suppose you can take a look. Just look," he said firmly.

She gave Cede another squeeze, then pushed him gently to the side and turned to Rock. His dark gray eyes stared intensely into hers while her fingers slipped into his short, brown hair, making her stomach do weird things. She slammed her eyelids shut and concentrated. Rock's brain was steadier than Cede's, much like his personality. He also smelled nicer, like a spicy cologne, probably because he had to shave whereas Cede still sported smooth cheeks.

"Well?"

How long had she been standing there, poking into his head? She dropped her fingers and stepped back. "Your brain is very steady. Cede's is bouncy, but they match your personalities. I think he's okay. Just keep an eye on him."

"You could keep an eye on me," Cede said, flashing big puppy-dog eyes at her.

"I have to get to work."

"Just for a little while?"

163

Rock smacked him on the head. "Stop begging. We're not dogs. Besides, she's a witch. She can't come."

"There's no reason I can't jog by, is there," she asked Rock. "I could run to the park with you. I was planning on turning around once I reached the park anyway."

"It should be okay as long as you don't do magic. I can't tell you're a witch right now."

He frowned a little and Honey wondered if he'd just realized he should be able to sense her magic since she'd just used it. She really should figure out how to adjust her air shield. Hopefully, he'd blame the light breeze for the lack of smell.

"Race you to that tree!" Cede said right before he took off.

"What tree?" she yelled, racing after him.

As she'd known he would, he declared himself the winner right before she caught up to him. Rock and the other wolf joined them, and they all continued on to the main road and finally the parking lot of the sports park. Already, the lot was full and people were parking on the grass wherever they could find a spot.

She'd wanted to watch the events for a few minutes, or at least run past them, but there were too many people and cars between the road and the playing fields. She'd be noticed. She stopped at the driveway into the parking lot. "I'll see you guys around. Have fun."

Cede grabbed her hand. "I wish you could stay."

"Me too, but if I want to have spending money, I need to work."

He pulled her into another sweaty hug before she could get away. She didn't mind, not really. She had the feeling that he didn't get a lot of physical affection from his new pack, or perhaps he wasn't yet ready for it. She, on the other hand, wasn't a wolf as far as he knew, and therefore safe.

"Rogues aren't allowed," a male voice interrupted.

Honey looked up to find two men and a woman, all in their early twenties and all in uniform, blocking the entrance of the parking lots. The one in the middle was the closest, so perhaps he was the one who'd spoken. She stepped out of Cede's hug and forward a little to put him behind her.

"Who are you talking to?" They should be able to smell that Cede wasn't a rogue anymore.

He sniffed at her and curled his lip. "This is a private event."

Oh, he was talking about her. "I wasn't planning on attending. This was just my turn-around point today."

He stepped closer, his nose twitching. "You don't smell like a wolf."

"No, I probably smell like sweat."

"You don't smell like anything."

"Oh, good. I guess my deodorant is working." She looked over her shoulder to Cede and his friends. "I'll see you guys around. Good luck today."

"What's this?"

Pain streaked across her upper chest and something snapped at the back of her neck. She looked down to the streak of red on her tan skin, then up to the necklace her grandmother had given her, dangling from the clawed finger of the bully in front of her.

"That is mine."

165

"Give it back," Cede demanded, trying to step around her.

Honey grabbed Cede's arm before he could lunge at the thief.

The thief sniffed at the charm and made a face. "It smells like magic."

"Because it is. May I have it back please?"

"You're a witch," he stated.

"Yes, and like I said, I'm out for my morning run. If you give my charm back, I'll be on my way."

He sniffed at the tip of his claw and made a face. "Your blood stinks."

"I didn't ask you to smell it." Was the charm making her blood smell like a lie since he was holding it?

"He scratched you?" Cede growled, noticing her chest for the first time.

"No Cede!"

She froze Cede before he could attack, then a split second later, froze the uniformed wolves too. She had a feeling they would try to arrest her for using magic on Cede even though she was protecting them. Plus, it made it a lot easier to retrieve her charm and wipe her blood off the leader's claw.

"What did you do?" Rock demanded while she tugged her broken necklace out of the stiff fingers of the middle guy. "Did you use magic on them?"

"He attacked me first and Cede was about to start a fight. It won't hurt them and it's temporary. They'll thaw in about twenty seconds. I'll refreeze them before I leave which will give us both thirty seconds to get away. Can you get Cede away from these guys and keep him away?"

"You're not supposed to use magic on wolves."

She pointed to her chest. "He attacked me first. Besides, this way no one else gets hurt."

He glanced down where she pointed. Something flickered in his gaze. "You should get that cleaned up."

"I will. It's not deep. Grab Cede. I'll unfreeze him first."

Cede was still growling when she unfroze him. Thanks to the grip the other wolf and Rock had on his arms, Cede wasn't able to spring forward at the frozen bully. He did try though.

"Cede, stop. They can't hurt anyone right now. I have to go. Stay away from these guys, okay?"

Cede gave another good tug. "He hurt you and stole your necklace."

Knowing how nice it felt as a wolf to be rubbed behind the ears, she reached up with her free hand and tucked some of his shaggy hair behind his ear, while letting her fingertips slide over his skin. He stopped trying to pull away and leaned into her hand.

"It's okay. I'll heal and I got my charm back. I'm going to go. You stay with Rock and away from these guys."

Cede looked to the frozen guy, then back at her. "He shouldn't have touched you."

"And now he's frozen and he's going to look really stupid with his mouth open like that until he thaws. Please, Cede? I don't want you to get into a fight and get kicked out of your new pack because of me."

He looked back at the bully and sighed. "Okay."

"Good. Freezing them again…now," she told Rock, then turned and ran.

She sprinted until she was back across the river into what she hoped was still neutral territory. It was a little further east than the climbing center, which she knew for certain was in neutral territory, but not that far off. She made it to the center in plenty of time to shower and get ready for her shift. For the rest of the day she kept an eye on the door, poised to disappear every time the door opened, but no wolves entered the building.

She was overreacting.

The guy had probably just wanted to make sure there weren't any witches around the park. There was no reason for him to seek her out. She'd had every right to freeze him.

Freezing Cede and the other two uniformed wolves was a different story though since they hadn't attacked her. She was pretty sure Cede wouldn't press charges. Hopefully the other two wouldn't even realize they were frozen. They'd just wake up and think they'd blinked or something, unless somebody noticed the three people standing like statues for thirty seconds at the entrance to the parking lot.

She should have thawed them sooner.

She jogged back to the school and sniffed for strange scents before entering. Nothing. Nothing new anyway. There was no one waiting to arrest her, which meant Cede and his friends hadn't mentioned where she lived.

She grabbed some food from the kitchen and jogged up the stairs to her room. The stench from a week's worth of sweaty work-out clothes greeted her. Yuck. She really should charm her laundry bag to trap the smell with an air shield or at least do her laundry before the next group of campers checked in tomorrow. First though, eat, then test her charm again.

She'd worked on her door-removal charm until well past midnight the night before. She knew it was unlikely that letting it set for a few hours would make it function properly, but she didn't know what else to try. If she couldn't get it to work she wouldn't be able to break into the Boston library or leave the magic sketch pad for the boys.

She tapped the charmed ring against a test pebble. It disappeared just like it was supposed to. She tapped the area again. Nothing happened. Ugh! She took a deep breath and let it out, slowly. Making things disappear should be as easy as making them appear, at least it always did when she transformed to her wolf and back. What was she missing?

21

I'M GONE

"Isabelle! Isabelle, wait."

She rolled her eyes, but she couldn't keep the grin off her face when she turned to meet Cede. His happiness at seeing her was always infectious and it had been over a week since she saw him last. Not to mention, she felt like celebrating now that she'd figured out the secret to getting her charm to work. She still couldn't believe it had taken her so long to think of attaching a magical anchor to things when she made them disappear. As a bonus, she could now make things appear and disappear just by touching them. She didn't need to transform to do it anymore.

"Hey Cede, Rock, new guys."

Cede jerked a thumb over his shoulder at the wiry guy and the taller one behind him. "Josef and Marc."

"Hi," Honey said.

"How's my head?" Cede said, stopping right in front of her and tipping his head toward her.

She put her hands on her hips. "You tell me."

"Lonely without you in it," he sighed, looking up through his messy hair with big puppy-dog eyes and a protruding lip.

"That's…you…ugh." She gave in and pushed her fingers into his hair. At least it was clean. She could smell the shampoo. "It's looking really good. I can hardly tell there was anything wrong." She retracted her fingers. "You going to run with me today?"

He shook his head. "We came to invite you to our Canada Day party tomorrow."

"He came to invite you," Rock clarified. "I don't think it's a good idea."

"What does your Alpha say?" she asked Cede.

"He said we can bring guests. I want to bring you."

"That's really sweet, but I don't want to cause any problems."

"Have you ever been to a Canada Day celebration before?" Cede countered.

"No."

"They'll be lots of food and games and fireworks. People will be everywhere. They won't notice you."

"Wolves notice everything. Speaking of, what happened after I left last week? Were there any problems?"

Rock snorted. "No, not really. They thawed and looked around, then stomped off somewhere. Their alpha requested to speak to Cede, but he'd disappeared by then."

"Disappeared?" she asked him.

Cede shrugged, "I was hot. I took a dip in the river."

He winked knowingly at her. Why would he…oh no. He'd hugged her when she was all sweaty. He'd gotten her sweat on him. Had he smelled her true scent? Did he know she was part wolf?

"So, you want to race?" Cede asked.

"Race?" she asked distractedly. Did Cede not realize what her smelling like a wolf meant?

"You will give us a head start, right?" Cede asked, winking again.

She widened her eyes at him, trying to convey her question.

He grinned. "I promise I won't say a word…or cheat."

He knew. Whether he knew she was a hybrid or just thought she was pretending to be a witch was a different question. Could she trust him? Too late for that.

"You mean give her a head start," one of the new guys corrected.

Rock snorted. "Ten dollars says she'll beat you to the turn up there."

The two guys looked her over suspiciously. "She can't use magic."

"I won't," she promised, forcing herself to stop worrying about Cede and join the conversation.

"Your own or any charms."

"I already gave you my word. If you're afraid, it's okay. Some people find me intimidating." Generally, the younger girls at camp, but she didn't add that.

He looked her up and down. "Right."

She wondered what he saw when he looked at her. A skinny kid with kinky hair perhaps?

"So, it's a bet?" She wiggled her eyebrows at him.

He squinted at her. "I don't trust you."

"Fine, we'll just race. Ready?"

172

A wonderful race-and-wrestle filled hour later, thanks to an over-exuberant, transformed Cede, she returned to the school sweaty, dirty, and perhaps ready to tackle Boston. Now that she had the charm, it should be easy, but what if something went wrong? Were there any details she was forgetting or other charms she should take?

"My goodness, what happened to you?"

Honey looked up to what, just a moment ago, was the empty entry hall but now hosted a lone woman right in the very center. There was no doubt in her mind that Ms. Charming set some kind of alarm charm whenever she was waiting for someone to show up.

"I went for a run."

"Did you fall?"

"Not exactly."

"Is that blood on your knees?"

Honey looked down at the crusty, dirty smears on her knees. Oops. She'd forgotten about that. She'd hit some gravel when she'd ducked and rolled to avoid one of Cede's pounces. "Maybe."

"Was someone chasing you?"

"Not anyone with bad intentions."

Ms. Charming frowned at her suspiciously. "Who then?"

Honey shrugged. "Some friends. We go running together and race sometimes."

"Mmm. Go get cleaned up, see the healer, then find me. We need to talk."

"Yes Ma'am." This wasn't going to be good.

"That was fast," Ms. Charming commented twenty minutes later when Honey walked into her office. "Did you see the healer?"

"No. There was no need. It looked worse than it was." Honey was wearing pants so Ms. Charming couldn't see that she had, in fact, already healed.

Ms. Charming sighed and pointed to the chair in front of her desk. "Sit down, Isabelle." She waited until Honey had complied, before speaking again. "I know who you are."

"What do you mean?"

"I know you're Rachel's granddaughter and I know the truth behind why your mother was killed."

"You do?" Surely her grandmother hadn't told Ms. Charming she was half-wolf. There was no way the woman would have allowed her in the school.

"Gaian Graves is a powerful enemy to have. I cannot keep you hidden if you insist on parading all over the city."

Gaian? Oh. Grandmother must have told her about Gaian and her mother.

"I am just another girl in a big city. Why would anyone notice me?"

"Dear, when it comes to witches, this is a small town. Everyone knows everyone else. You may not have met them, but the witches will know about you. Gaian has offered a reward for information on your whereabouts."

"Did he give a reason for wanting it?"

Ms. Charming frowned at her. "No, just that you were a suspect of interest in a murder investigation and not to approach."

Honey gritted her teeth and balled her hands into fists. "He's claiming I murdered my own mother?"

"He didn't say who was murdered."

"What do you want me to do? Do you want me to leave?"

Ms. Charming sighed and spun in her chair so she could see out the window. "Isabelle, you are one of the most impressive students I've seen in a long time. You work hard, you study hard, and you're very responsible, but you are too noticeable. There's no way I can keep you hidden here. In fact, I wouldn't be surprised if someone has already reported where you are. I'll get a message to Rachel and..."

"There's no need," Honey stood, "I'll leave right now."

"I didn't mean you had to leave now, just soon."

"It's okay. I don't want to cause any problems and if the witches are as knowledgeable as you think, it's dangerous to wait."

"You have someplace to go?"

"Yes. I know of several places, none as good as this one, but they will be safe. Thank you for letting me stay here. I learned a lot."

Ms. Charming opened a drawer on her desk and pulled out a small white envelope which she placed on the desktop. "This is the money your grandmother gave me for your tuition. You earned your keep while you were here, so it's yours. Also, I will spell you and your ID so you can get a ticket out of here without anyone being the wiser. I can change your name too, if you think it would help."

"Do you have a charm for that? I need to stop by the climbing place and let them know I can't work there anymore and they will expect me to look like me."

"I'll take care of it. Go get your things then come here so I can spell you."

Honey ran up the stairs. She had more clothes now than when she'd arrived, mostly gym-related things for work. It was too much to stuff into her two bags, but she had a new trick up her sleeve. She stuffed the most essential things into her backpack and the rest into her duffel bag and a pillowcase, then stashed the duffel and the pillowcase in what some books called a pocket dimension and others called the nether. She preferred 'nether' since things in pockets wouldn't just float away the way unanchored objects seemed to do.

She was about to open the door to go downstairs when a whisper that sounded like Ms. Charming's voice slipped into her ear, "*They're here. Escape if you can. I'll try to distract them.*"

Honey retrieved a portacorn from the front pocket of her backpack and took a step to the side to stand in front of the wall next to the door. Where should she go? One of the boys' rooms? Nathan's would be good because he didn't have any siblings at home. Wouldn't he be surprised. On the other hand, it was the end of June and a Sunday. There wouldn't be many people in the library at VU at this hour and this time of year. It might even be closed right now. She could hang out in the bathroom and wait for the National Council Library to close, then enact her plan.

She squeezed the acorn in her hand and pictured her destination. The cold, cement-dust odor with a hint of ozone that signaled the formation of a portal reached her nose before her eyes caught the tell-tell waiver of the wall. She knew Ms. Charming probably wouldn't hear it, but just before she stepped through, she whispered, "Thank you. I'm gone."

22

BOSTON

Honey pulled her hood up to hide her face and very carefully peeked out the bathroom door. Except for the moonlight coming in through the big windows and the motion-detecting light in the bathroom behind her, the top floor of the Vindale library was dark. Good. She slipped back into the bathroom and shut the door. Time to don the disguise she'd put together so she could save the charm her grandma's friend had given her for an emergency.

The movies always showed the heroes and the bad guys dressed in tight clothes. That really made no sense because then the cops or whoever was looking for them would be able to guess their weight and height and how they moved. She added a bulky over-sized pair of sweatpants to her hoodie, then pulled a thin black balaclava she'd purchased at a sidewalk sale over her tightly braided hair. After putting on enough make-up to compete with Emo batman, she slipped on the really creepy, polarized, full-face mask shield she'd bought from a gag store. It looked like a giant lens from a reflecting pair of sunglasses. She turned away from the mirror with a shiver. No one would recognize her wearing that.

After making sure her portacorn and disguise charms were in her pocket, her new 'nether' charm was on her finger, and her grandmother's I'm-a-witch charm was still pinned to the inside of her bra, she slipped out of the bathroom. The main room of the human library likely didn't have a motion-sensor in the middle of the room, but she tried to stay in the darkest parts of the darkness while she crept to the yearbook section to slip one of the Magic Slates into the yearbook where she'd found her mom. Liam was smart. He'd be able to decipher the coded message she planned to remail him.

Next, she crept back past the bathroom to the janitor's closet. It wasn't locked. She feared that might mean the entrance to the library had moved again, but as soon as she reached for the back wall, a familiar blue spark shot out to greet her. It was probably her imagination, but it felt like the library was glad to see her.

On impulse, she put her hand on the wall before she stepped inside and whispered, "Library, if you can understand me, don't tell the librarian I'm here. It's important. I'm trying to break a curse."

The library didn't respond.

Oh well.

She stopped for a moment to breath in the ancient scent she thought she might never smell again. Like the non-magical library she'd just left, the only light in the magical one came from somewhere above, presumably from the moon, although she couldn't see any windows on this side of the door. Placing each footstep as gently as she could, she made her way around the metal walkway and down the metal stairs all the way to the bottom floor. She'd never seen the librarian send or receive any books, but she had seen her go into the room next to the main room for maps. It seemed like the most likely place to start her search for the portal doors.

Again, the door wasn't locked. Honey carefully pushed it open and stepped inside. Light flared. She froze with one foot still raised above the floor. After several moments, when nothing moved except the flickering flame on the large candle in the center of the room, she slowly put her foot down. Okay then. Magical motion detectors must be a thing. She just hoped the library hadn't called the equivalent of 911.

Shelves covered the two long walls on either side of her. Not surprisingly some of the shelves held books, but the majority had boxes of scrolls and random items like vases and tea sets and sculptures of metal and gears that looked like they belonged in a steam-punk museum. A large, heavy-looking book stand, bigger than the one at the witch school, occupied the center of the room. An equally impressive tome lay closed top of it. Power radiated off the book and the shelves, tempting her to look around, but she focused on the wall beyond the pedestal. That wall was bare except for five portraits, nearly identical in size, that formed a row right at the perfect height for portalling books. That, and the tell-tell cement dust smell of portals made her certain she'd found what she was looking for. Which one went to Boston though? None of the little golden nameplates under the photos said anything about

Boston. How was she supposed to get through? Maybe ask?

"I need to send a book to Boston," she declared.

Nothing happened.

Maybe the pictures were clues to the locations. She took a closer look. One she recognized as Victoria Wixx, her own ancestor. Another was Victoria's brother, Anthony. His plaque said, *Anthony Servious Wixx, Tremontaine, 1630*. That wasn't right. She knew for a fact that he was alive in the mid-1800s, unless he had a much longer lifespan than normal witches. Victoria's plaque said *Victoria Madeline Wixx, Fountain Colony, 1872*, yet in the portrait, she looked younger than she did in the picture of her from the 1850s hanging in another part of the library. Also strange was that all the portraits had place names she'd never heard of.

York 1834 under a third portrait sounded familiar. Where had she heard that before? Did it mean New York? No, she was pretty sure New York had been called New York long before 1834. Plus, she'd never been to New York, yet she remembered seeing the word 'York' somewhere recently. She closed her eyes and willed the word to appear like she'd seen it before. Right, it was from a display in the London library. Toronto wasn't always called Toronto. It was once called York and had served as Canada's capital until 1867 when Ottawa became the capital.

So, if that door went to Toronto, 1630 was likely Boston because Boston was one of the oldest cities in the US. Had it once been called Tremontaine?

No time to look it up. She needed to work fast before the librarian showed up. Besides, she could always pop back if she was wrong.

She reached forward and tugged on the frame. The picture didn't move.

Was there a spell holding it shut? She lifted her face shield and sniffed around the edges of the picture. Other than the portal, she didn't detect any spells but…what was that? Chocolate? Salty snacks? Books. The smells clustered under the bottom middle part and top corner of the frame. That must be where the librarian touched the frame to open it.

Honey ran her fingers along and behind the picture where the scents were strongest. Nothing. She tried again, reaching even further around. At the bottom midpoint of the frame, her middle finger touched what felt like a wire. A click sounded and the portrait swung open, releasing a strong scent of cement tunnel.

Now came the scary part. Could she insert and retrieve just part of her body or not? Bracing herself for possible pain, she slowly inserted her left pinky finger into the wavering spot on the wall. It didn't hurt. She pulled it out and checked the tip. It was still whole. She stuck her finger in again until it completely disappeared, then pulled it back out. Ha. It was still there and other than a pulling sensation, it didn't feel too odd. So far, so good. Now to open the door on the other side of the portal. She turned the charmed nether ring on her finger so that it faced forward and thrust her fist into the wall.

Her fist sank in up to her wrist, then stopped. Had she already reached the door on the other side? She thought it

182

would be farther. Was it possible that there was something already in the portal? If so, was it safe to use her ring? She shook her head. Nobody would just leave a book in a portal. She tapped the blockage twice with her ring. Nothing blew up, but she was suddenly able to move her hand even farther. She pushed in up to her elbow before pulling her arm, whole and unharmed, back out. This was going to work! Time to enact the second part of her plan.

She stepped back a few places, then ran forward two steps and leapt hands-first through the chest-high portal. A moment later, she rolled to her feet in a much more contemporary-looking room with three rows of small metal doors across the wall she'd just come through and panes of glass that looked out into the main library on the other three. The library hub looked exactly like the picture in the book she'd read except everything was dark save for the exit lights over the doors and random lights along the ceiling that she guessed were smoke detectors.

The library book on libraries had described the main public part of the library as a three-story U-shape that wrapped around the less-public central hub, offices, and research areas. The forbidden texts were above the hub on the second floor in a room accessible only by a single door. That is, unless you could make things disappear, like she could.

Although she hadn't tripped any lights when she arrived, she was certain magical cameras were already recording her every move and an invisible stop-watch was ticking down somewhere. Moving quickly, she dragged a small, sturdy-looking table away from one of the glass walls and jumped on top. Luckily, the ceiling was low enough for her to reach. She hadn't thought of that. With a tap of her index finger, the ceiling tile above her head was gone, leaving the floor of the room above. She concentrated on making only a few feet of the floor above her disappear and touched the surface with her middle finger. Darkness appeared above her right before the smell of ancient, dark-tainted magic poured over her. Other than that, no alarms went off and nothing seemed to be happening around her either. This was too easy.

She peered harder up into the gloom above. There *was* some kind of spell. Her brain interpreted it as red laser beams like they had in all the spy movies except these were arranged like a fence instead of random lasers. The beams smelled hot too, like the coils in a toaster. No doubt if she touched it she wouldn't live long enough to regret it. It looked a little like the barrier around her grandmother's covenstead. She might be able to tease it apart wide enough to get through, but she needed to be able to walk across the floor. How could she disable it without setting off an alarm? Could she use little mirrors to redirect it? She rolled her eyes at herself. First, she didn't have any mirrors, and second, they would interfere with the lines and likely set off the alarm.

The lasers looked solid rather than smoky like a lot of spells, almost like a real fence. Hmm. She'd never tried it before, but maybe she could send a spell to the nether with the ring. Spells weren't strictly molecules, but they were something. If this worked, maybe she could simply send Zavier's curse to the nether.

No. The curse might think she owned the nether. That would be bad.

Okay, she needed to focus. If she used the ring, it would either work, she'd set off an alarm, she'd destroy the ring, or some combination of those. What would she do if any of those happened? If she set off the alarm, she'd give up and go back through the portal. If she destroyed the ring, well, she'd give up and go back through the portal.

But first, she jumped back off the table and tapped the ring twice against air near the floor to pull the portal door out of the nether. There. Even if she couldn't stick the door back in place when she left, at least the witches couldn't claim she stole it. She leaned the door against the wall, then looked around for something to put the ring on just in case the grid was also electrified. Pens! She grabbed a regular-looking one with a cap and clip, then hopped back up on the table.

With the lightest of touches, she tapped her ring against the red laser line. It sizzled but didn't melt or explode. She quickly tapped it again, hoping it hadn't already destroyed her magic. To her amazement, the red lasers disappeared. That worked? She sniffed. The hot filament smell was gone but the stench of nasty magic had increased. Was it really that easy? She slipped the ring off the pen and tossed the pen up through the hole. It clattered to the floor somewhere above, but nothing else happened. Okay then. Here went nothing.

She jumped up, caught the edge of the floor, and pulled herself up. All the climbing she'd done recently made it easy. Before she forgot, she scooped the pen up off the floor, because only an amateur would leave clues like that, then looked around. If she'd been human, it would have been pitch dark, but her wolf senses atop her magical ones enabled her to see shapes and faint auras around some of the books. It wasn't nearly enough to read by, but she was prepared for that. She whipped out the camping headlamp she'd picked up at a hardware store and put the band over her balaclava so the light was above the face shield. Luca would double over laughing if he saw her.

"Okay, where are you?"

The room stank of every nasty thing she could think of – dead bodies, sewers, body odor, skunks, feet, hatred, fear, despair, dread. She would have held her nose if she could reach it. Breathing only through her mouth, she turned her head slowly, sending a broad beam of weak light onto the nearly full bookshelves that lined the walls and the five podiums scattered around the room. The book was unlikely to be there, considering how long it had been in the library, but she checked the podiums first. Four were empty, but the one center middle had a book open to a gruesome picture of a hand-drawn skeleton with entrails stretched out beside it and smelled like death. She backed away. Mr. Witthem's magic smelled, but not like that.

Starting by the door, she began systematically inspecting the shelved books. Nearly all of them were more than a foot tall and several inches thick with hardback bindings, some elaborately decorated, although only a few displayed recognizable letters. Each book had a label stuck to the edge of the shelf beneath it with a series of letters and numbers, but nothing that formed words. It looked a little like the Dewey decimal system but without the decimals. She stepped back and looked around for a catalog, but nothing stood out. It must be stored elsewhere. *Looking* at every book on the shelves would take a long time. Maybe smelling would be faster? Starting by the door, she walked past the shelves, pulling the air toward her nose, searching for the scent of the Mr. Witthem's magic. She gagged a few times from the smells, but she hadn't had time to eat, so nothing came up.

She was beginning to despair that it wasn't there when, in the back corner opposite the door, she caught a whiff of unwashed human body and blood that she would recognize anywhere.

"Found you."

She reached for the rather plain, brownish-green book, then thought better of it and used her eyes to check it for spells. A greenish film slithered over the cover that reminded her of the curse on the land, but no red lasers or other indications of a library alarm were visible.

"Did you curse your book too, Mr. Witthem? You really were diabolical."

She jogged back over to the door and picked up the pair of gloves she'd seen hanging there. They looked like simple cotton gloves, but the shields she smelled on them were strong. She slipped them on and ran back to the corner. Excitement and nervous anticipation thrummed through her when she reached for the book. She'd finally learn something useful that could help her break the curse, assuming the book didn't blow up in her face or something. She touched the spine with only one finger first. The cloudy film swirled around her finger but didn't try to go up her arm. Embolden, she worked the book off the shelf and set it on one of the book holders.

Like the spline, the front cover of the book was undecorated save for a raised circle in the middle. The film of the spell bubbled and spread out of the circle like the white fog created by the dry ice she had dropped in water in the chemistry lab. Who was the curse for, the people who touched the book with their bare skin, or those who opened it? She guessed opened for no reason other than that's what her gut was telling her. It was a nastier blood curse than the one on the land. Despite the other horrible smells in the room, she sensed pain and despair.

Zavier thought she was a curse breaker, but how was she supposed to break this?

She asked the book.

It didn't talk.

In her mind, she reviewed everything she'd read and the spells she'd broken. Maybe she could pull the curse off like she'd removed Frederica's curse. She made a grabbing motion, but instead of a cloak, a golden rope appeared in her vision, tying the book shut, with the ends glued together under a big seal in the middle of the book over the circle. The seal had channels that reminded her of the channels in the blood tester. Could it be that easy? Did she dare use her own blood on a cursed book?

According to everyone else, as a hybrid she was already cursed, unless she truly was a curse breaker, then it shouldn't affect her, right?

She took off one glove, transformed the tip of her index finger into a wolf's claw, then stabbed her thumb.

"Mom, Dad if you're watching, please stop me if this is the wrong thing to do."

She felt nothing either for or against while she extended her hand over the book. Just in case, she waited a few seconds before finally squeezing her finger.

"With the magic in my blood, I destroy your curse, Mr. Witthem."

She probably didn't need the words, but she felt the need to say something before she flicked her finger and exposed herself to the world, maybe.

Her aim was off, but her blood changed trajectory and fell directly into the center of the seal. The one drop split into eight more that flowed with amazing speed through the patterns that wound and twisted around the circle and then toward the edges of the seal where the golden rope was anchored. Black, inky shadows started to crawl over the edges of the seal toward her blood.

"I don't think so."

She extended her palm over the seal and envisioned the molecules and the force between them pushing the black back so that her blood could reach the rope. The black fought, but she'd been practicing with shields. She conjured miniature ones that blocked the black from crawling any closer to the center and even pushed it back.

The moment her blood reached the edges of the seal, gold zipped over the red. Gold flashed and the seal and the ropes disappeared. The smell was gone too, mostly, at least she thought it was until she put her face closer to the cover and pulled the air under her face shield. Had the man never washed his hands?

Whatever. She straightened and wiped her already healing bloody finger thoroughly on her dark hoodie before she put the glove back on. Finally, she could get what she came for! Watching the book closely just in case there was another spell set to go off when she opened it, she lifted the cover to the first page. A single word in the center of the page, written in letters six inches high scoffed at her.

HA!

She turned to the second and third pages, then flipped through the rest of the book, all the way to the last page. Every single page was completely blank. She sniffed them and looked for spells – nothing. Unless the witch had used a human invisible ink trick, which she doubted because he was witch, the whole book was a ploy to trick people into thinking there was some hope of breaking the curse. Had the people who'd opened the book before her seen the 'HA!' too, or had the curse taken effect before they got that far?

Going after the book had been a waste of time, and now she had to escape before she was caught.

She put the book and the gloves back, turned off her headlight, then stuck her head back through the hole in the floor. Still no alarms or movement. Either the National Library wasn't as securely guarded as that book on libraries had implied, or there was something nasty waiting for her somewhere.

She slid through the hole feet first, then did her best to tap her charm in the exact same spot she'd tapped it before. The red grid reappeared above her head. She tapped the piece of flooring back in place. Promisingly, it didn't immediately fall on her head. Just in case, she quickly replaced the ceiling tile. Since no one was chasing her, she took the time to put the table and pen back.

Next, she touched her ring to the portal door still leaning against the wall so she could magic it back into place once she was was through the portal. Now all she had to do was dive back through. She was about to do just that when she had a disturbing thought. What if the librarian was waiting on the other side of the portal or had shut the door? If she was waiting, she might notice if a finger came through the wall, but if something small flew through, she might not see it, or even better, it would distract her.

There wasn't anything useful in her pockets, the pen on the table might work though. She picked it up and removed the cap. No one would miss a cap. With a flick of her wrist, she sent the cap flying through the open portal. It didn't bounce back. The way was clear.

Somewhere in the building, a red light began flashing.

"Seriously?"

She dove. Right before her head entered the wall, white light flashed, leaving the ghost of an image on her retinas.

The room in Indiana was dark. The candle had been extinguished, she assumed automatically, since it flared to life again when she straightened. Spotting the pen cap near the podium, she scooped it up and returned it to Boston, then stuck her hand and the ring wrist deep into the portal and tapped it twice. She felt something solid appear, but whether the door would stay in place was another story.

A door creaked behind her.

"Stop right there!"

The molecules froze around her. Her adrenaline was pumping so fast, she not only unfroze the molecules, she sent them shooting all over the room, making the candle flicker. Moving quickly in case the librarian was already sending more spells at her, she dropped to her shoulder and rolled so that she ended in a crouched position facing the door. The librarian gasped and took a small step back, although she didn't lower the hand with the freeze-stone that was clearly not working. The fright on her face melted into resolve and she backed away to stand inside the door of the portal room, then touched the frame.

"You won't be able to leave the library, thief, even if you get past me."

Honey froze her, then strode forward and plucked the stone out of her hand. The librarian had come with it ready, and she was still in her pajamas, very comfortable looking ones with little flying witches. Honey wondered where she'd found them.

A better question, she thought shaking her head to get back on track, was how the librarian knew she was here. There was no reason for the alarm to go off here, nor did she hear one, which meant there must be a silent alarm that connected the libraries. There went her plan to conserve her other portal by jumping to another library. She could still lay a fake trail though. She unlatched the York portrait, stuck her hand through the portal, and made the door on the other side disappear. Just in case someone was there, she tossed the freeze stone through, then tapped her ring against the air a few inches farther in through the portal than where the door should be. There. They couldn't claim she'd stolen anything if the door was there.

Now she just had to get out of here. "Library, I swear I didn't steal anything. I broke into the other library and broke a curse. That's it. I didn't harm the Librarian either. She'll unfreeze shortly. I have to go. They'll kill me if they catch me."

The second fat candle on the other side of the large podium in the middle of the room flickered to life, illuminating the librarians frozen face and gaping mouth. Since there was no one else there, Honey addressed the room.

"You want me to see something?"

Pages fluttered on the podium. Honey slipped closer. The large book on top looked an awful lot like the ones in the forbidden library but unlike those, it smelled clean and powerful, like a cluster of power lines. She froze the librarian again before she started reading.

It is done. The curse is laid. I will take my piece as far north as I can travel.

The pages started flipping and stopped near the middle of the book. The handwriting was smaller and neater.

I have retrieved our piece. I will take it to the new world and . . .

The pages flipped again, but not far. It looked like the same handwriting.

It is stamped in metal. It is too fragile to be left to the elements. We have begun construction on a grand house with a stone foundation. What better place to hide it?

Honey was expecting the flipping this time. The book stopped at some loopy writing that was smeared in places.

They killed my sweet Emeline and her newborn child. There was nothing wrong with either of them. Henry was her mate. How could he be her mate if the pairing was unnatural?

The pages turned again to a very slanted set of words.

If you are reading this, you are the one I have foreseen. I found our piece and I will melt it down. You must find the other four pieces. Only then will the curse be broken. The families you seek are the Lamberts, Brights, and Evelstone. The fourth name is lost to history, but perhaps the other families have record of it. You will be betrayed. Take care.

Beneath the lines was a drawing of a thin diamond with shapes that could be words etched around the outside.

"Now!" the librarian shouted.

Shoot, she'd forgotten to count. She froze the librarian again. Why she'd yelled, Honey had no idea.

The candles on the podium blinked out, but another candle on the shelf to her right lit up.

"You have something else for me to see?"

She hurried over to the shelf where a smallish book wiggled at her. She felt like she was in a Harry Potter movie as she reached up to pull it out. The book tilted and the small section of shelving beside it swung in to reveal a dark space that smelled of old dust.

"You want me to go in there?"

Another flame popped to life in the gloom.

"Okay. You aren't the one who's going to betray me, are you?"

The candle on the shelf flicked off rapidly, like she'd offended it.

"Sorry. I didn't mean to offend. I trust you."

She stepped inside. The shelf immediately swung shut behind her, leaving her in a narrow, dusty space with cobwebs and a small lamp hanging from a hook.

Behind her, there were popping noises and bangs and yells. Come to think of it, it had been really odd that no one had tried to come through the portals to capture her while she was reading the grimoire.

"Did you keep them away?" she whispered. "If so, thank you."

Another flame appeared, even further into the gloom. She tapped her face shield to send it to the nether. It was dark enough already in the room without it.

"I'm guessing you want me to follow the lights?"

Very, very far away another flame appeared.

"Following the lights I will go."

23

TUNNEL'S END

Who was going to betray her? Who could she trust? How long was this passage? It went on and on, much farther than made sense for the size of the university. She hoped it ended soon. She was getting hungry, like dangerously hungry, and there wasn't any convenient pizza to steal.

"I sure hope this ends where I can buy some food, or at least find some," she amended. "It must be pretty late."

Conveniently, a door appeared in the light of the next flickering flame. Had the library been waiting this whole time for her to tell it where she wanted to go?

"I don't suppose there's a mirror somewhere? I must look pretty scary."

There was no mirror.

She couldn't go out dressed as she was. If the witches had her on camera, she'd be easy to spot and the makeup she'd smeared on her face was going to make her too noticeable.

Would it though? What if she removed the balaclava and replaced the sweatpants with leggings? She could keep the hood up to hide her hair and most of her face.

197

She made the adjustments to her wardrobe, stashed the balaclava in the nether where it wouldn't be found on her person, and put the money she'd taken from Gaian months ago and a couple of twenties her grandmother had given her in easy reach in the front pocket of her backpack since that was the only US money she had.

"How do I look?"

A candle flickered to life right by the door.

"I'll assume that means acceptable. Thank you for your help." She put her hand on the handle, "Don't let the librarian get in too much trouble if you can help her. She did her best."

She wasn't sure what she'd see when she opened the door, but it wasn't the bottom of a ditch and walls of scraggly trees. Up a slope, about two-hundred feet away, an all-night convenience store glowed in the dark.

"Wow. That's perfect. Thanks again. Hopefully I'll be able to come back and visit."

She got the distinct impression the library wasn't keen on that idea, although it didn't boot her out or anything. She stepped out the door and shut it firmly behind her. The door wasn't there when she looked back.

From the clustered lights in front of her and the darkness beyond, she deduced the library had spit her out on the edge of town near the not-so-busy highway. There was only one other customer in the store when she walked in. Keeping her face down, she grabbed enough snacks to fill up her half-empty backpack and her stomach, then walked up to the register behind the bullet-proof glass. The guy who'd been looking at lottery options the whole time stepped into line behind her. Before she could shift over to keep him in her sight, something cold and round pressed up against her head.

"Give me all the money or I'll blow her brains out!"

Really? The one time she really didn't want to get noticed, some idiot pulls a gun on her? It was a big gun too, which meant she had plenty of real estate to grab it and shove it upwards while she jabbed and kneed him in all the places that hurt the worst. He fell to the ground, clutching his groin with his gun-free hand. After that it was easy to jerk the gun away. She froze his arms and hands where they were, but not the rest of his body, so that he was still moving in the footage sure to be on the security camera. The gun she pushed underneath the bullet-proof glass toward the attendant, while at the same time willing her magic to make any finger grease she'd left on the barrel disappear. Keeping a careful eye on the criminal, she began collecting the snacks now scattered all over the floor.

Meanwhile, the attendant, a middle-aged woman with a messy bun, had come around the counter to train the gun on the thief.

Freezing the guy hadn't done her any favors. Honey was barely keeping herself from tearing into the packages.

"Can I give you $40 for all this and we call it even?"

"Cops are coming."

"I don't want to be here."

The woman glanced over at Honey and the mound of food on the counter. Honey automatically refroze the would-be thief's arms. "Sure Hon. Grab one of those fancy smoothie drinks too. Vegetables are good for you."

"Thank you."

She pushed the $40 as far under the glass as she could, sending any fingerprints on it to the nether, then stuffed everything she could into her backpack and grabbed a green-colored smoothie bottle. The flashing lights were a block down the road when she jogged out of the store and back into the trees.

There were no other good options. She'd have to use her second portal. She pulled out the second portacorn and stood in front of a wide tree while picturing the one place she was pretty sure no one would look for her.

24

YELLOWSTONE

Honey stood and shook out her fur, agitating the dust particles dancing in the rays of light streaming in through the cracks around the old wooden door. She snorted to get the dust out of her nose, then transformed into her human form. The large snack bag with fruit and nuts satisfied her hunger, but she wished she'd thought to purchase some water. No matter. Zavier would have some.

Taking advantage of her human height and thumbs, she opened the shed door. A moment later, she was a wolf again and all her belongings were safely tucked into the nether. She shivered. Despite her fur, it was chilly outside, much chillier than she expected for July 1st.

Although it was still early morning, she had to hide behind bushes or dip down into the grass several times to avoid being spotted by cars while she made her way along the road to the hotel. Yellowstone looked much different without all the snow, but there was only one road, so the motel where Zavier and his pack worked wasn't hard to find. Once her destination was in sight, she jogged into the center of a handy cluster of trees and popped into human form. For the first time in nearly two months, she purposely removed the charm her grandma had given her from her person and sent it to the nether.

Thankful she had the hoodie, both because of the chill and because it helped hide any vestiges of the emo makeup she might have left from last night, she strolled into the lobby while looking up just enough to see who was at the front desk. It wasn't Maya. A young man, a wolf she didn't recognize, looked expectantly up at her. He didn't smell like Zavier's pack either. She ducked her head.

"Good morning, may I speak to the manager please?"

"Is there something I can help you with?"

"I don't think so. Zavier is still the manager, isn't he?"

What if he wasn't? Where would she go?

"Are you here to seek his help?"

"Maybe."

"Have a seat over there," he pointed to a row of comfortable-looking chairs against the wall. "He comes in at 8."

"What time is it?"

"Seven."

"Oh." She was so close to seeing someone she knew, but so far. "Is his beta here?"

"Which one, Ruth or Walter?"

Ruth was a beta too now? Good for her.

"Walter."

"Walter is."

"Really?" She realized she was grinning up at him from under her hood and quickly dropped her head again.

"Yeah, I'll page him. Have a seat. It might be a few minutes."

She tried to sit. It was literally impossible to do so without squirming. She finally gave up and started wandering around the lobby, pretending she was interested in the rustic art on the walls.

She smelled Walter's clean scent before she saw him. He strolled in looking tall and leggy in Western-style jeans, a plaid shirt, and a healthy tan. Western looked good on him. "Someone wanted to see me?"

The guy at the front desk nodded toward her. "She did."

She could tell the moment Walter recognized her. His whole face lit up with a grin. "Hon.."

She cut him off with both index fingers to her lips.

"..w can I help you?" he quickly adjusted.

"Can we speak in private somewhere?"

"Sure. Follow me to the office."

He didn't look back at her the whole way down the hall, but the moment he shut the door behind her after she'd stepped into the small room, he pulled her into his arms and spoke into the top of her hood, "Oh my gosh, Honey, where have you been? We've been so worried."

She soaked up the hug and gave him just as big a one in return. "Canada, learning how to be witch. I can do so much more now."

He released her enough to look at her, but still gripped her upper arms lightly. "Really?"

"Yeah, watch." She touched his jacket and made it disappear, then pulled it back out of the nether. It hung on him just like it had before she'd removed it.

"Wow."

"And I can make a charm that does the same thing. I was thinking wolves might use it to stash their clothes, but I'm still perfecting it."

"How did you get to Canada? What happened the last day of school? We were all worried when you just disappeared. Brayton was frantic. We thought you'd been kidnapped until Alpha Silver sent a message saying you were with a friend."

"I *was* kidnapped. I escaped." She told him the whole story, everything but her mother's last name and the fact that there was a witch library hidden inside the college library. She made it sound like she'd had four portacorns when she talked about breaking into the Boston library.

"So now every witch in the world is looking for you?"

"Apparently."

"Why didn't you call us and let us know you were all right?"

"Messages can be intercepted, and cell phones don't work in a magic school. I mailed Nathan a cypher and you the message in case someone was watching the mail so we could meet at a designated time in an incognito message server, but it must have gotten lost because you guys didn't show." It brought tears to her eyes thinking about it again.

Walter pulled her into another hug. She loved his hugs. "Oh, Honey, I'm sorry. Nathan said he got something odd, but I haven't seen my mail in weeks. Mom is supposed to forward it to me, but she keeps forgetting."

"That's okay. I'm here now."

He leaned his chin against the top of her head. "Yes you are. Are you sure no one can follow the portal?"

"Yes. I read a book on them."

"You can stay with our pack then."

She shook her head against his chin. "No. I have things to do. That's why I came here. I think I know how to break the curse on the land."

"But you said the book was blank."

She couldn't help the grin on her face while she shared what she'd realized only this morning.

"Yeah, but I broke the curse on the book and it was just like the one on the land. It's a blood curse and the only way to break a blood curse is with blood more precious than that used to make the curse in the first place. I don't consider my blood to be more precious than that of the woman who died, but the magic might. I am the only curse breaker to exist in over a hundred years, after all."

"You sure you're a curse breaker?"

"Yeah. I read a lot of books in Canada and I definitely broke the curse on that book."

He gave her another squeeze. "So why didn't you break the curse last night, since you slept there?"

"I didn't want to break it and then have someone buy the land out from under Zavier. I want him to buy it in my name before I try to break it. That way, even if it fails, you guys can still use the land. The curse won't affect me because I'm a curse breaker. I think that's why I survived the other curse too."

"Honey, no. We can get along without it."

"Your pack is growing. You need it."

"I don't think we have enough money saved yet."

"Alpha Silver might help."

"We can't put it in your name," he tried again. "You're in hiding."

"Not Honey Smith, no. I don't have any IDs for that. My current name is Isabelle Winters, but we probably shouldn't use that either. I don't think the magic cares what I'm called. It will know who I am. How fast can a person get a fake ID made?"

"Honey, no. It's a bad idea."

She lifted her head off his chest and stepped back from him far enough to put her hands on her hips and glare. "Walter, it needs to be broken. If I can do it, I'm going to do it. Who knows when or if another curse breaker will be born."

"You can wait until you have more experience."

"Every witch in the world is after me. I might not get another chance. They're going to figure out which book I looked at eventually. We need to get this done before they figure it out."

"Come in," Walter said loudly to a soft knock on the door.

The door creaked open and a familiar face appeared at the crack. "Hey Walter, Milo said there was someone to see me?"

"Zavier!" Honey screeched.

Her cousin's mouth dropped open, but he had the presence of mind to shut the door before he said her name and pulled her into a hug just as tight as Walter's. He even spun her around.

"I think I know how to break the curse," Honey grinned.

"Excellent, what do we do?"

"It's too dangerous," Walter insisted.

"Tell me the plan and then we'll decide."

25

BRAYTON

"Good afternoon, Alpha Silver."

"Good afternoon, Luna Lynn. May I come in?"

"Of course. To what do we owe this pleasure?"

From the kitchen, Brayton saw Alpha Silver wave a finger at the wolves with him, indicating they should stay on the porch. That could only mean one thing, at least he hoped it did. He waited for the door to close, then stepped into the open entryway.

"Did you hear from Honey?"

"I did."

"How is she? Where is she? Is she okay?"

"She's fine."

"Brayton, why don't you go see if your father is free. Alpha Silver, can I get you something to drink?" his mom asked politely.

"No thanks, Lynn. I'm actually in a bit of a hurry. I just came to pick up a few of Honey's things."

"Why?" Brayton asked.

Alpha Silver grinned, "So I can take them to her."

"I want to go."

"Brayton, I told you to get your dad," Mom snapped.

"It's okay. There's no need to bother him," Alpha Silver said.

"Where is she," Mom asked.

"I'll tell you, but everything I say stays in this house. Don't tell your friends anything over the phones or the computers."

"Why?" Brayton demanded.

"Because Honey believes the witches are listening in, which is why she hasn't contacted you."

"That's ridiculous," his mom said.

"She was kidnapped by the witches. They found her somehow."

"What!" Brayton snarled.

"Calm down, boy. I'm not the enemy," Alpha Silver frowned at him, then turned to Brayton's mom. "A kind witch helped her escape. She's been in Canada, working."

"Why didn't she call us or send us a letter? Something?" his mom asked.

"Like I said, she was worried the message would be intercepted. She did attempt to contact the Little boys but she didn't know Walter was in Yellowstone and he never got her message."

"Why would she contact them and not us?"

Mom was trying hard to hide it, but she was hurt. Why had he been so awful to Honey when she first joined the pack? Stupid.

"She and her friends had discussed secret messages and she sent the message in code. She was hoping they'd remember what they talked about."

"Why would the witches kidnap her? Is this because of the library in Texas?" Brayton asked.

"No. It has nothing to do with Honey. It's because of her parents."

"Her parents?" his mom asked.

"Yes. Don't ask me to explain. It's the reason her mom was in hiding."

"Let me guess, her mom did something to piss off the witches?" Brayton said.

"You could say that."

"Do you know what she did?" his mom asked.

"Yes, but I'm not at liberty to say."

"Does Honey know?" Brayton asked.

"She does now."

"Where is she?" Brayton asked.

"With Zavier. The witches have put out a reward for information on her whereabouts. She was...she met some witches in Canada and didn't feel safe there anymore, so she fled."

"The poor girl," his mom said. "How did she contact you?"

"Zavier had a florist deliver flowers to my wife with the phone number to a burner phone, so I called her on *my* burner phone which Honey insisted I buy months ago. Matt taught her all sorts of tricks." He looked at his watch. "I have a plane waiting for me. Honey asked me to get her backpack and to make sure and leave her phone here."

"How are we supposed to contact her then?" his mom asked.

"I'll give her your numbers. Part of the reason she didn't call was because she didn't know them and she was afraid to search for them online."

"May I come?" Brayton asked.

"Mmm, I don't see why not unless your parents have some objection."

"Take him. He's been mooning about the house all summer."

"Pack quickly then. Five minutes."

"Yes, Sir."

He was going to see Honey! He felt like he was flying instead of running up the stairs. He stuffed a handful of underwear and whatever pants and shirts were in his drawers into his backpack, then ran into the bathroom for his toothbrush. After throwing in a hat and one last shirt, he walked into Honey's room. Mom had put all her things away except for the backpack which lay in the middle of the desk. It was still full of her books. Knowing her, she probably wanted to reread the books. He tossed the bag over his shoulder, lifted his own, and ran down the stairs.

His parents were waiting with Alpha Silver in the entryway.

"You don't have her phone, right?" Alpha Silver asked.

"Uh." He had no idea where Honey's phone was. He hadn't cared since he found it ringing in her dorm room without her there.

"I've got it right here," Mom said.

"Good. I'll drop by when I get back and give you updates. Remember, do not mention Honey or anything to do with her over the phone. I'm on a business trip to look at some land Zavier found," Alpha Silver said.

"Will you tell my friends where I went?" Brayton asked his mom.

"Of course. Go. Tell Honey I miss her and to stay safe."

The sun was still shining when they landed in Cody, Wyoming. He knew it was silly to be disappointed it was Walter and not Honey waiting for them in the airport, but he was. Alpha Silver and the three wolves with him piled into a black rental SUV. Brayton opted to ride with Walter in his old truck. Maybe he could finally get some answers to all the questions rattling around in his brain.

"How is she?" he demanded the moment Walter climbed in and slammed the door.

"Fine."

"How long has she been here?"

"Just since last night."

"How did she get here?"

Walter shot him a glance when he put the truck in gear to back up. "What are you, a cop?"

"No, I just want some answers."

"You can ask Honey. We'll be there in a few minutes."

It felt like a lot longer than a few minutes before they finally parked in front of a sprawling farmhouse with multiple outbuildings and a pile of construction supplies in the front yard. Ruth was waiting in the doorway to greet them, but not Honey. Where was she? He made himself wait for Alpha Silver to park and climb out. Ruth stepped forward to greet them and apologize for Zavier's tardiness before finally turning to lead them inside.

"You okay Brayton," Walter asked beside him.

"Yeah, why?"

"You are giving off some strange vibes."

"Vibes?"

"You know what I mean."

"No, I don't. Where's Honey?"

Walter frowned at him. "I don't know. Let's find out."

They didn't have to go far. Alpha Silver only made it a few steps in before Honey ran from a dark corner of the room and wrapped her arms around him. Brayton felt a strong surge of jealousy, but quickly tamped it down. Alpha Silver was her uncle. Of course she was happy to see him.

"Hey Honey."

She lifted her head from Alpha Silver's shoulder and started at him with wide eyes. "Brayton?"

"Yeah."

"What are you doing here?"

"I brought your backpack." He held it out to her.

"Wow. Thanks." She released Alpha Silver and moved to take her backpack from him. He pulled it back.

"Don't I get a hug?"

"You want one?"

He spread his arms. "What do you think?"

"Yes?"

"Come here, you." He grabbed her arm and pulled her in. Her delicious scent surrounded him and he sucked it in. All the tension from the plane ride and the past two months vanished like magic. The cavernous hole in his chest was suddenly filled to overflowing. He laid his cheek on top of her head and pulled her even tighter. "I was so worried about you."

"I'm sorry. I didn't mean to worry you," she mumbled against his chest.

"I know."

He closed his eyes to better enjoy the sensation of her in his arms.

"Brayton, you can let go now," Walter said.

"I could."

Honey squirmed and lifted her arms to loosen his grip. "Brayton!"

Reluctantly, he opened his eyes and let her go. That's when he realized everyone in the room was watching him. "She gives good hugs," he said.

"Mm-hmm," Alpha Silver said, frowning at him.

"So, Honey, what did you need your backpack for?" he asked while casually letting her go.

"This." She went into the small living room to the right of the door and started pulling everything out of the bag. After she had a neat pile of books and notebooks, she stuck her hand back in and pulled out a handful of cash cards and a small, dark blue book.

"Is that a passport?" he asked.

"Yep." She opened it and grinned.

"Are you going somewhere?"

"It's always good to be prepared." She stuffed the cards and the passport in the front of the backpack and started shoving the books back into the main pocket. You guys hungry? Ruth and I made supper."

26

PROPOSAL

She'd been right to make breaking the curse a priority. Zavier's temporary pack house was packed and chaotic. Kids were everywhere, running and hiding and yelling. As soon as Zavier strode in though, they all quit whatever they were doing and rushed to greet him. The younger ones swarmed him with hugs while the older ones lingered until he'd at least acknowledged them. Even the adult members popped out of wherever they were to say hi.

"It's like a harem," Honey heard Brayton mumble under his breath.

"Jealous much?" Honey whispered back.

She helped Ruth serve food to the kids, then scooped up some chili for herself and settled next to Alpha Silver to eat since he'd save her a seat. Brayton, oddly, plopped down right across the table from her, then popped-up when she did and volunteered to help with the dishes. He'd never volunteered once to do it in his pack in all the time Honey had been around him. Stranger still, he insisted on playing a board game with her and Walter and the older teens although he'd always claimed they were too boring when she and her friends had a game night at college.

"What was Canada like?" he suddenly asked right after she'd finished her turn.

"Lovely." She launched into a description of the running trails and the climbing gym and the university and the library, of course, and how nice the weather was.

"But where did you stay?" he asked.

"A friend's place."

"What friend?"

"Witch I met while I was there," she hedged. Why was he so nosy?

"You stayed at a witch's house!" the girl with long, straight black hair sitting on the other side of the table asked with shock, but there was admiration in her eyes.

"Sure. They're people just like us, and I worked with all humans at my job."

"What about the local packs?" Brayton asked.

"The house was in neutral territory, plus I helped a rogue find a home while I was there. We became friends after that."

"I wish I could see Canada," Maya sighed.

"Maybe you will someday." Honey said. She was certain Zavier would take her if she asked, but would Maya ever ask? "I will say though, that I missed my friends, so if you go, take your friends with you."

"Did you miss me?" Brayton asked smoothly.

Why on Earth would he care?

"You *are* a friend," she said to be polite.

After the game, Zavier pulled her and Alpha Silver into his office. She eagerly told bio-dad her plan, certain he'd loan her money to buy the property. She was absolutely shocked when he stamped her idea with a flat-out, "No." No matter what arguments she presented, mostly all perfectly sound ones, he just shook his head. She took it back. He was nothing like her dad-dad. Her real dad would have at least considered it. After all she'd done and all the effort she'd put into learning about curses it was infuriating. She couldn't stand to be in the room with either of them anymore.

"Why won't Alpha Silver and Zavier let her try?" Brayton was asking Walter right outside the door when she jerked it open.

"Because they don't think I can do it," Honey fumed, slamming the door against the wall as she stormed out. "I broke into a freaking library to do this for Zavier and he's gone chicken."

"Whoa, hold on there, Honey." Walter grabbed her arm and pulled her to his chest. She leaned against him and relaxed into his familiar scent.

Brayton made a sound that might have been a growl.

"You know it's because they care about you," Walter soothed with his chin on her head.

"I know. I just really wanted to help you guys and your pack. It's stupid to wait. As soon as the witches figure out what I looked at, they'll start watching for someone to buy the land."

"They'll give up eventually, then you can try."

"Besides, it makes so much more sense for me to take the risk," Honey continued like Walter hadn't said anything. "The pack needs Zavier. No one needs me."

"I need you," Brayton blurted.

Honey blinked at him in surprise. "For what?"

His mouth opened but it took a few moments for him to finally say. "You're a good sparring partner, for one." Brayton grabbed her hand and jerked her out of Walter's arms and into his. "And you're very cuddly with that sweatshirt on."

She'd ended up with her back to his chest and his arms around her waist. It *was* a nice thick sweatshirt, but still, "Walter is a good sparring partner and he's cuddly too," she pointed out.

Brayton nuzzled the side of her head, "But you smell better."

"I'm right here," Walter said, "although you're right, she usually does smell better, and she is a very good hugger, which, I believe, she was in the process of giving me before you so rudely ripped her out of my arms." He took Honey's hand and jerked her back toward him.

She ended up facing forward into Walter's chest, so she hugged him back.

Brayton, to her surprise, grabbed Honey's shoulder and tried to jerk her back toward him. Oh. They were trying to make her feel like she was important by fighting over her. How sweet. She planted her feet.

"Stop it, you two. I know what you're doing, and I appreciate it, but the fact is, no one is depending on me like they do Zavier."

"How much does the land cost?" Brayton asked.

218

"Seventy-five thousand," Honey informed him.

"That's it?"

"Yeah."

"How many acres?"

"Over two hundred."

"Wow. That *is* a good deal."

"I know!"

"What if I bought it?"

Honey lifted her head from Walter's warmth to see Brayton more clearly over her shoulder. "You have seventy-five thousand dollars?"

"More, actually."

"Would you put the land in my name? I did a little research on Walter's phone. I can have a power of attorney signed so I don't even have to be present."

"Stop right there," Walter demanded. "Neither Zavier nor Alpha Silver approve of this idea, Honey."

"But Brayton out-alphas them because he's in my pack."

"I'm sure Alpha Brandon won't agree either."

"My parents encourage me to make investments," Brayton informed him. "Why do you want it in your name, Honey?"

"Because I think it will be easier to break the curse if I own the land."

"And what happens if you fail?"

"Then we can sell it back to the bank. You'll probably be out a few thousand, but I can pay you back once I find the account my dad started for me when I was a baby."

"And she might have bad luck and get caught by the witches again," Walter said.

"Shall I list all the ridiculous challenges she's already overcome?" Brayton said. "College at fourteen, straight A's in said college, won the MMA championship as a freshman, probably would have won the OA championship too if she hadn't been injured, and do I need to mention her SAT score? She did all that while facing a series of personal challenges that I wouldn't wish on my worst enemy. If she says she can do it, I believe her. Besides, I'll be with her the whole way. I'll protect her."

"You can't fight the witches," Honey said, "they'll spell you."

"Not if you give me some of those charms of yours. You have some protective ones, right?"

Honey realized she was gaping. "Really? You'd use them?"

"I'd be foolish not to."

What had gotten into him? First, he offered to support her idea and give her money, then he was willing to wear a magical charm when she knew for a fact he hated magic. Maybe he was more of a friend than she'd realized. She stepped away from Walter and wrapped her arms around Brayton. He truly wasn't a bad hugger and she wasn't complaining about his stomach-flipping body spray either.

"Thank you."

After several long moments, he released her and pulled out his phone. "I'll make some calls."

27

THE CURSE

"Everything is ready," Brayton said, walking into the large family room where Honey was playing with baby Mika. "We just have to meet with the bank representative on the property and hand over the check."

"No," Alpha Silver said. "This is a bad idea Honey. As your…"

"Uncle?" Honey interrupted. "Brayton's mom is my legal guardian and she said it was okay."

"Did she," Alpha Silver asked, looking directly at Brayton. "Did you tell her everything?"

"You know I couldn't. I just told her I found a great deal and I was investing in some property."

"Did you tell her it was cursed?"

"I'm not stupid."

"Could have fooled me. Do you know how many other people have eyes on this property, how many other packs? Even if you are able to remove the curse, Zavier and his pack won't be able to live there. They won't be able to defend the land. They're actually safer here, in the middle of the humans."

"But they won't own the land. I will, or Honey will," Brayton argued. "If other packs attack the land my pack will defend it, plus, we can always sell it again for a ridiculous profit if Honey gets rid of the curse. I'll even split the profits with Zavier since he found the land."

"You are proposing to drag your pack into a war thousands of miles away from your pack lands? Did you mention this to your dad?"

"Yes. My dad supports what Zavier is doing and has agreed to send people to defend the land if needed."

Honey handed Mika the toy he'd thrown on the ground. Why was everything so complicated? All she wanted to do was provide a safe place for women and children who needed it and the men were talking about a war.

"Where is Zavier? Did he get smart and decide not to be your power of attorney?"

"He had to go to work, Alpha Silver," Honey said, "but he'll be there in time for the signing. You're going to come with me, right? I know the perfect place we can hide while they walk the property lines, plus Brayton can text you the moment the land is in my name. I'll get to work on the curse before it realizes I'm the new owner."

"Honey, your mother…"

"Is not here. She would help these women if she could though. So would Dad."

"Not if it meant you were in danger."

"I'm always in danger."

Bio-dad threw his hands in the air. "Gah, who knew teenage girls could be so stubborn?"

"Pretty much everyone in the world," Brayton mumbled under his breath, then louder said, "You two should go now and get in place."

"Oh, wait," Honey dug into her pocket and pulled out what looked like small hair bands with dangling little hearts. She offered one to Brayton and four to Alpha Silver, one for him and one for each guard that would be with them. "These are shield charms. I put them on elastic bands so you could wear them around your ankles in wolf form or just keep them in your pocket in human form. They activate automatically if they detect magic being used against you. I'm not sure how long they'll last, but they should be good for a few minutes at least. I gave one to Zavier too."

"And you have one," Brayton said.

"Yes, I have one," she agreed. Of all the people she knew, she was still not sure how to process that Brayton was the one person who had supported her plan as soon as he heard it. She kept catching him watching her too, and every time, instead of looking away, he would give her that lop-sided grin that did strange things to her insides. "I'm going to change."

Honey left Mika with the woman who was watching all the smaller children and ran upstairs to find a bathroom to transform in. Walter, Zavier, and her dad knew about her odd transformations, but Brayton didn't and she didn't want to risk him finding out she was a wolch and backing out of the deal.

Bio-dad and his guards met her outside in wolf form and hopped into the back of the rental SUV. Brayton and Ruth got in the front. Brayton dropped Ruth off at the motel for her shift, then turned off the main road onto a dead-end road a few miles away from their destination to let them all out.

Brayton stepped in front of Honey just before she jumped out. He put his hands on her shoulders and his forehead against hers. "Be careful, okay. If you don't think you can do it, then forget about it. I don't care if I lose every cent. I'd much rather keep you safe."

It was so sweet, she licked him, and not a gross, all over your face kind of lick, just a little one, on his cheek. He gave her one of his stomach-flipping grins and kissed her on her cheek. He'd always kissed her on the forehead before. What did it mean when an alpha kissed you on the cheek? She made a note to ask Walter.

It was the first time she'd ever gone on a run with her bio-dad. He took the lead in front of her. His three guard wolves surrounded her so that she was in the center of a diamond. It was like running with Brayton but without the paw signals. Boring. If bio-dad wasn't helping her against his better judgment, she'd do something to make it more fun, like nip at the tail threatening to whack her in the face. At least it was nice outside.

It didn't take them long to get into place in the bushes that lined the creek close to the middle of the land. An hour later, Brayton and Zavier appeared in the old truck with Walter driving, followed by a big black car. A round man and a slim, 30-something woman in a perfectly fitting suit and sneakers stepped out of the car. Honey couldn't hear them from where they sat, but it wasn't hard to imagine what was being said. They introduced themselves, then the round man asked where Honey was and Zavier explained that he was power of attorney. The woman must have protested because Zavier pulled out the other form Honey had signed stating she was aware of the curse and all the failed attempts to remove it. They'd decided to use her real name since it was associated with the wolves, and came up with a story that Honey had found a witch who might be able to break the curse. The woman either didn't know about witches or she was very familiar with them because Honey clearly saw her say, "What witch."

One of the guards with her nudged bio-dad's shoulder and pointed his snout towards the north. Bio-dad shook his head. Honey scratched a question mark in the dirt. Her dad replied with a circle with two triangles for ears. He was good at stick figures. She gathered him to mean there was another wolf watching, but that wasn't surprising. There were lots of real wolves around.

Brayton and Zavier and the bank people started walking around the property. Honey plopped down on her belly and forced her tail to keep still. Waiting was always the worst part of anything. After a very long time, at least forty-five minutes, everyone returned to the vehicles. The round man spread some papers on the hood of his car and Zavier applied a pen. Honey didn't need the buzz in the doggy saddle bag one of the guards was wearing to know the deed was signed. Zavier and the round man smiled and shook hands. The woman, on the other hand, was standing on the far side of the car with her back to them while slowly scanning the property.

Honey had a sudden urge to stand and shake, which would be stupid because the woman would likely spot her or the dust. Was that what the curse did – encourage people to do stupid things? She nearly erected a shield around herself, but that would be stupid too, the woman might be able to sense it. And transforming to tell her dad she could feel it? Beyond stupid. The guards would know she wasn't normal. Even writing it like she suddenly wanted to do could cause repercussions. Nope, the only thing to do now was stick to the plan.

She waited for the car to depart before she stood and did not shake. She should run up and thank Brayton and Zavier. No, no, no, stupid curse. She had to get it out of her head. It might be the curse telling her to put a shield around her head, so she'd expose her magic to bio-dad's guards, but ha, she was wearing still wearing her anti-scrying hairband. If anyone asked, she would just point to that.

She imagined a solid helmet over her head. One of the guards shot her a look. She lifted her paw to show the hairband on her wrist. She really should have made herself a protection charm, but there were only so many hearts in the package.

She couldn't smell or see anything suspicious, but maybe that was the curse talking. She wrote '*sense anything*' on the ground. Bio-dad shook his head.

Jogging, not sprinting, she made her way to the pile of rocks that served as a grave. The curse smelled stronger than she remembered. Was that because it was now aimed at her? With her paws, she began pushing the stones away. It was much harder to move rocks in wolf form, but she soon had a small piece of ground exposed where the pearls were. With her second sight, she could see the curse surrounding her and battering at her shield and almost thought she could sense its frustration. Good, that meant her shield was working.

The guards couldn't witness the next part. She glanced at bio-dad and made a twirling motion with her paw – turn around. He barked and the three guards disappeared in different directions, hopefully to scout and not to secretly watch her. Brayton and Zavier were next to the truck, obscured by a large evergreen. If the wolf was still spying, he wouldn't be able to see through the trees either.

She wiped the pad of her left front paw and the sharpest claw on her right hand against her fur to clean them, then stabbed the center of her palm. If what she'd read was right, it would only take a drop or two of her blood to counteract the cursed blood. She extended her paw over the space. A couple of thick drops splashed into the dust between the pearls. Like it had on the grimoire, her blood started spreading much faster than should be possible, but instead of channels, this time it was in little grooves in the dirt. They wound and twisted into the outline of a head with long hair splayed out to the side. The rest of the blood disappeared under the stone where she guessed it made the rest of the outline. Abruptly, the whole outline turned gold. At the same time, a darkness started seeping in just like on the book. This time though, her blood wasn't the only thing fighting. A faint blue came from the interior of the woman's outline.

Honey had a sudden, brilliant idea.

"*You didn't want to die, did you? You fought him. You were a witch too. Why didn't I think of that before,*" Honey thought at the shape. "*I will break your husband's curse, but would you like to help me set up something better? Will you protect the women here?*

227

They have been hurt like you. Will you protect all those who live and visit this land from those who would do them harm? I'm not asking for another curse. I just ask that you block their entry or any spells or weapons and if they are inside when they decide to do harm, to still the molecules around them until they can be removed. Do you agree?"

The blue glow pulsed. "*Okay. I will introduce you to their other protector as soon as I'm done.*"

The black had grown thicker while she was talking. She conjured up shields and pushed it away from the gold of her blood which was attempting to flow toward the borders of the land. The black fought back, moving to slip around the edges of her shields. She was going to have to fight it the whole way? Well, she'd known it wasn't going to be easy. She followed a gold line toward the border while concentrating on keeping the black away. Either the curse was pretending it was faltering as she went or it actually was, because by the time she reached the border, she felt like a snowplow charging through a single inch of the fluffy stuff. She was vaguely conscious of other wolves beside her while she ran along the border, urging the gold into place but she didn't dare look up. She didn't want to miss a single tendril.

A lot faster than it had taken the bank people to walk, she completed the circle. The moment the golden ends joined, the black cloud started shrinking toward the center of the property, becoming darker and thicker. She chased after it and reached it just as it coalesced into the form of a man with his arms extended like he was casting a spell. Without hesitation, she leaped. She'd never attacked anyone with her teeth before, but the smoke-man deserved it. The awful taste of unwashed body, brimstone and oddly, sadness, filled her mouth when her teeth pierced the thick fog where the man's neck would have been. Imagining she was biting a pillow and not some smoke-man, she shook her head hard enough to release feathers. The smoke dispersed. Instead of landing on a shadow body, she landed on the ground.

It was really hard to spit in wolf-form.

She ran into one of the outbuildings and changed, then spit.

"Honey, are you all right?" Brayton called from just outside the door.

She spit again, then stepped outside. Brayton was in the process of taking off his shirt, probably to hand to her. "I'm fine."

He gaped at her. "Where did you get clothes?"

She grinned at him. "There are charms for all kinds of things."

"But how did you get dressed so fast?"

"Like I said…"

Zavier swooped in, grabbed her, and spun her around. "You did it, didn't you?"

"You can tell?" she asked her cousin dizzily when he finally sat her down.

"I saw that black thing you attacked disappear and the whole place just feels better and smells better, a little like you, actually."

"Excellent. I have someone to introduce you to, though."

"Who?"

She took a step forward and realized her legs had gone boneless. Zavier's fast reflexes saved her from falling flat on her face.

"Honey, are you okay?"

"A little tired. I'll have to sleep for a while, but I need to do this first."

He scooped her up. "Where too?"

"Back to the rock pile."

"The witch's wife?" he guessed while he carried her across the yard.

"Yes. I got rid of the original curse but I left her protection. She has agreed to keep out everyone who means harm and freeze any who get past her borders. You'll just have to carry them out."

"You did that? Oh, wow." He hugged her to his chest, then kissed her temple. "Best cousin ever."

28

JULY 4

Honey opened her eyes and stretched. The air outside her thick blanket was pleasantly cool. She didn't recognize the room though. It looked like the interior of a small barn or maybe a shed. A bottle of water and an energy bar were sitting on a cardboard box next to her cot. A second cot with a sleeping bag was along the wall at the foot of the cot she lay in. She sat up and downed most of the water in one long sip, then ripped open the wrapper on the bar. Her stomach felt cavernous. How long had she been asleep?

Outside the thin walls, she could hear the high-pitched squeals of children and the deeper, calmer tones of men and women. Bright sunlight leaked through the cracks in the wall and under the door which meant she'd slept through one night at least. Where was she? She threw off the blanket and was pleased to find her shoes waiting when she put her feet on the floor.

The ill-fitting plank door with a wooden latch opened onto a grassy yard full of people with a long, low building behind them. Ah, she was still on the cursed land, well, not cursed any more.

"What's going on?" she asked the first woman she came to.

"Oh good, you're finally awake. I'll get Alpha Brandt."

"Wait, how long did I sleep? What day is it?"

The woman turned and answered while walking backwards. "It's the Fourth of July. You woke up just in time."

"Just in time for what?"

"For the party," Walter said behind her.

Honey whirled around. "Hi, Walter."

"Hi, Honey," he opened his arms, "want a hug?"

"Always," she said, diving into them.

"Mmm, you smell like sleep and magic. I never thought I'd like the smell of magic, but I like the smell of yours." He released her. "You should probably change your clothes though, we have guests, and fix your hair."

She reached up to pat her head and made a face at what she encountered. Her hair had mostly come loose from the hair band that had held it in the braid and was sticking out in all directions. "How silly do I look?"

"Silly isn't the word I would use. Go get fixed up and I'll grab you something to eat. How many platefuls do you want?"

"Funny."

"I'm serious, pizza thief."

"You're never going to let me live that down, are you?"

"Never," he responded with a playful seriousness that made her giddily happy. She had the best friends.

There was something she had to take care of before she did anything else though. "What are we using for a bathroom?"

"Currently, there's just the outhouse, but there should be a few port-a-potties arriving momentarily."

"Nice."

"I know. Those are the first things Zavier is planning to install, a well and a septic tank. He's also talking about using the hot water from the hot springs to heat the house and maybe the hot tub for when we get the resort built."

"I was asleep for one day and you've already got the plans made?"

"Zavier started making plans as soon as he saw the land. Designing things and making them all work together is like a hobby for him. I've learned a lot since I've been here."

"That's great."

"Yeah, I'm thinking of transferring out here, then I could help on the weekends."

"I didn't realize there were any schools close to here with engineering degrees."

"Montana State is less than 200 miles away."

She wrinkled her nose. "That's not close."

"It's closer than Indiana. We can talk later. Go get cleaned up before Brayton realizes you're awake."

"Why, what's wrong with Brayton?"

"He's like a mother hen. He freaked when you passed out after introducing Zavier to the witch and he slept on the ground outside the door of the shed all night. He'd probably still be there but Ruth insisted she needed some muscle to help her start moving things into the house.

We've already had the chimney inspected. The roof needs some patching, but as long as it's not raining, we'll be fine."

"Why did you put me in the shed, not that I minded."

"Alpha Silver thought it would be safer and Zavier agreed. We haven't seen any witches."

"Good."

The outhouse was surprisingly clean. Someone had even added flowers.

Back in the shed, she pulled her duffel bag out of storage and put on fresh clothes. They probably smelled like magic too, considering she'd last washed them in the basement of a magic school, but at least they smelled cleaner.

"Honey, are you in there?" Brayton asked through the door.

"Hold on."

She didn't want to put her dirty clothes in with her clean ones but she didn't want to leave them out either. She pulled the pillowcase from the nether and quickly moved things around before putting it all away.

"What's up Brayton?" she asked, opening the door.

He reached out and gently squeezed her shoulder. "You okay?"

"Yeah. I'm fine."

"You sure?"

"Yeah, why?"

The grip on her shoulder tightened and his eyes hardened. "Oh, no reason. I just put some property in your name that carried a terrible curse and shortly after signing the papers, you fainted and slept for over twenty-four hours."

She shrugged and pushed off his hand so she could step back and let Walter pass with the two huge plates of food he was carrying. "Curse-breaking takes a lot of energy. That really smells good, Walter."

"I know. Ruth is an excellent cook."

"Didn't you just recite some words or something?" Brayton asked.

"There was a cost, Brayton. That wasn't an easy curse to break."

He stayed mercifully silent while she took the first bite of succulent melt-in-your-mouth barbecue. Her taste-buds screamed in appreciation. "Mmm, that is so good."

"What did she do, steal some barbecue this time?"

"Liam! Luca!" she squealed, but not so exuberantly she dropped her plate. That, she carefully placed beside her before leaping up to wrap an arm around both of them. "I missed you so much."

Memories of all the weeks alone, thinking she might never see them again, or that they were glad she was no longer around, surged along with a tidal wave of tears.

"Hey, hey it's all right Honey-bun, we're here. We missed you too," Luca said, patting her on one shoulder.

"Come here, Pumpkin." Liam pulled her to his chest.

"That's just great guys, surprise her when she's sungry," Walter scolded behind them.

"Sungry?" Luca scoffed. "That's not even a word."

"It is, I just made it up. Sad and hungry."

"I'm not sad," Honey sniffed, and wiped her cheeks while still leaning against Liam. "I'm just overwhelmed."

"What would that be, hungerwhelmed, whungered, overhungered?" Luca asked. "Hmm, I'll have to work on it. Can I have my own, personal hug now?" He extended his arms.

"Always." She gave him a quick hug. Quick because the barbecue smell was making her mouth water so bad she was about to drool.

She released him and backed toward the bed. "Okay, I really, really need to eat, so tell me why and how you are here while I chew."

"The why is easy. Because you're here," Luca said.

"The how is by car," Liam said.

"But how did you know I was here?" Honey asked after she'd swallowed a huge bite. "Walter, you didn't tell them did you?"

"Don't worry, I told them in code."

"What code?"

"He texted that he'd found the pepperoni thief," Luca grinned.

She rolled her eyes, then scooped up another huge bite of food. "This is really good."

"The noises you're making kind of clued us in," Liam teased.

"Before I forget, Nathan said to tell you he wanted to come, but his internship doesn't allow for vacation days," Luca said.

"Tell him I miss him too and give him a hug from me when you get back."

"You're going to have to give me another one because I'm not giving away mine," Luca declared.

"So, what did we miss," Liam asked, sitting beside Honey on her cot. Luca sat down on her other side and almost immediately started playing with her hair. Darn Brayton, he'd distracted her before she had a chance to brush it.

Walter recited the whole story, keeping the witchy details to a minimum due to Brayton's presence. Brayton, for some reason, was leaning on the wall next to the door with his arms crossed, glaring at her. She pretended she didn't notice.

"And then this dark figure appeared. Honey attacked and tore out its throat," Walter said. "It was just like a movie, but the special effects were real."

"The taste was real too," she shivered and took a bite out of her corn.

"Was it the witch's ghost?" Luca asked.

"No, I think it was his essence. I could see his wife's too, but not like his. Hers was a shape on the ground where she died. She agreed to protect all the people who lived on this land. I introduced Zavier to her so she would know him."

"She talked?" Luca asked.

"No, it was more like I felt her agree and her shape glowed stronger for a moment." She looked up at Brayton, "I should introduce you too, just in case something happens to me. Zavier is going to list you as my beneficiary tomorrow as soon as the office opens."

"Why should something happen to you, Honey? What did your mom do to anger a witch?"

Honey pretended to be all consumed with acquiring more food by handing Liam her empty plate and pointing to the other one sitting on the box. Liam handed her a napkin and mimed wiping his face, and then offered her the plate. The napkin came back with more sauce than a girl should ever have on her face.

Embarrassing.

"What about the curse, did you feel it at all," Luca asked.

"Yeah. It kept urging me to do stupid things, like stand up and basically wave at the witch the bank representative brought with him."

"She was a witch?" Brayton asked. "I couldn't smell it."

"Pretty sure," Honey said.

Luca handed her the end of the braid he'd fashioned and leaned on her shoulder. "I'm so glad you're safe."

"Me too," Zavier said from the doorway. "Wow, it's crowded in here."

"Honey Smith Silver, what are you doing in a shed with four boys?" Alpha silver said behind him with his fists on his hips.

"Eating."

"Don't you have any female friends?"

The nose-tingling smell of cement and ozone started wafting from the wall next to Luca.

"What the…" Luca got out before a frizzy haired girl stepped out of the portal, followed her father.

"Isabelle! See dad, I knew I could do it."

Honey lowered the buttery, fluffy biscuit she'd been about to chomp. "Frederica? What are you doing here?"

"You are my portal lesson for today, how to portal to a person instead of a location." She looked around curiously. "Where are we?"

"Are you in trouble Isabelle?" Mr. Felix demanded, all serious. She wasn't sure what he was going to do with his hand palm up that way, but she guessed it wouldn't be good for her friends.

"No. These are my friends, Luca, Liam, Walter, Brayton, Alpha Silver, and Alpha Brandt."

"Two alphas?" Frederica squealed. "I didn't know they could get along long enough to stand that close to one another."

"Sure they can."

"I'm Frederic Felix, portal master, so don't think you can attack us, I'll send you to the Antarctic," Frederica's dad warned.

"Mr. Felix, it's fine," Honey said. "They have nothing against witches. In fact, it's thanks to a witch that we're all here. There's a party. You guys want barbecue?"

Honey could smell how nervous Frederica was while she and Zavier showed her and her father around, but Frederica acted like it was normal for two witches to be walking in the middle of wolf territory. Her father, on the other hand, was understandably confused and protective. Zavier ignored the witch's gruff behavior and started detailing what he hoped to build and why.

"Can you feel it?" Zavier asked after they'd made it around the house to the hot springs and back.

"Feel what?" Mr. Felix snapped.

"The shield. Honey, Isabelle to you, broke the curse on this land and convinced the woman whose blood was

239

spilled to set the curse to protect the women here instead."

Honey had been wondering how to address the fact that she had two names. Trust Zavier to just blurt it out, but would it be safe?

"No."

"Hmm. I think I can smell it, but maybe that's because I knew what it smelled like before."

"How exactly does Isabelle know you?"

"She broke a curse a witch put on my head," Zavier said before Honey could explain anything. "She saved my life and now she's provided me with land for my pack where we had none before. Ah look, more guests. Mr. Felix, these guys are big, but don't be nervous. Alpha Henry gave me a chance when I first got here. I invited him over for some barbecue. I doubt he'll stay long. He has his own pack to party with. The Fourth of July is a big holiday here. Uncle Rory, come on, I want to introduce you."

A huge pick-up with a crew cab pulled into the yard. Four big men spilled out. Zavier left Honey and her friends to walk towards the largest of the men with a huge grin and his arms wide. The man looked so stern Honey was afraid for Zavier, but his stony face cracked into a big smile complete with big, shiny white teeth when Zavier reached him and they shared both a handshake and a man hug.

"You did it," the big man sniffed, "Ze curse is gone."

Zavier had never mentioned Alpha Henry was from Russia, not that it mattered, but Honey did appreciate a good Russian accent.

"My friends did."

"I don't suppose I convince you to sell?"

"It's not mine to sell. I found a very generous landlord. Besides, this place needs a lot of work before it will be profitable."

"You vill give me opportunity to invest?"

Zavier slapped Alpha Henry's broad shoulder. Honey wondered if Alpha Henry even felt it. "Of course. None of this would be possible without you. I'm still looking into the logistics of building a resort or hotel, but I will need investors at some point and you'll be the first man I see."

"Good. Now vhere is zis barbecue? Ruth's cooking is legendary."

"He's making deals with the Russian mafia," Mr. Felix muttered under his breath.

"No he's not," Honey said quickly. "Alpha Henry gave Zavier a job when he first got here when most of the other alphas refused to see him. He also hired the women that have joined Zavier's pack. It's a very unique situation. Most other alphas would never allow a new pack to come into being on their property. If he's Russian mafia, he's only shown his good side to Zavier."

Maya jogged up with Mika on her aproned hip. "Honey, can you watch Mika for a few minutes? I don't want him underfoot while we're serving everyone."

Honey put out her arms. "Of course."

"Let me have him," Luca demanded a few seconds later. "You're holding him wrong."

"I am not holding him wrong. I could hold him upside-down and he'd be happy."

"Just give in," Walter said. "You know how Luca is around babies."

"You like babies?" Frederica asked with surprise.

"He comes from a huge family," Honey explained, handing Mika over. "He introduced me to his mom and she immediately started making wedding plans and offered to watch our children. It was frightening."

"She didn't realize you were so young," Luca defended.

Mr. Felix frowned, "She wanted her son to marry a witch?"

Could he not feel she was a wolf or were there so many wolves around he couldn't tell? Interesting.

"She didn't know I was witch," Honey explained.

"Isabelle, can I have a word, privately?" Mr. Felix asked.

"No," Brayton spoke for the first time since her witch friends had arrived.

"What's it about?" Honey asked.

"Those portals I gave you."

"We can speak here. My friends know about them."

"Did you use them?"

"Yes."

"Where did you go?"

"I went to a library in Indiana and then I portalled here."

"What did you do in the library?"

She smiled at Liam. "I left the magic slate for my friend to find. If I'd known I was going to see him in a few days, I would have kept it with me."

"That's all you did?"

"Well, I did do a little research to figure out how to break the curse on this land, but that's it."

"Research?"

"Yes."

He gave her a very parental look. "Did this research involve breaking into a library by any chance?"

"Maybe, but I didn't take anything. I just read a book."

"Isabelle, you broke into a heavily guarded facility. You've got half the witch-world looking for you."

"They won't know who I am unless you tell them. Besides, I already had half the witch-world looking for me. The witch who murdered my parents put a price on my head."

"What?!"

"I would have gone through normal channels if I could have, but with him chasing me, I wasn't sure how much longer I'd be around to break the curse. I didn't get you into any trouble, did I?"

"No, but what are you talking about? There's a price on your head?"

How could she make him understand? "Yeah, I was in a kind of witness protection program in Canada but he found me. I escaped with your portal, so thank you for that."

"Does he know you're a curse breaker?"

Brayton was frowning at her or him or both. Maybe she *should* have had this conversation in private.

"I don't know. He tested my blood the last time he caught me but I think he just wants me dead."

"Why?"

"Because of my mom."

"What did your mom do?"

"Marry my dad."

Mr. Felix shook his head, then pulled something out of his pocket and offered it to her. "I probably shouldn't give this to you, but if my daughter was in trouble I hope someone would help her." He pulled back his hand and gave her a little glare, "but promise me that you will not break into any more libraries using my portals."

"I will not break into any libraries using your portal."

"Know that I can find you any time," he warned.

"Really?" She grabbed at her braid to make sure her hair band was there, "even with anti-scrying and anti-seeking charms?"

Her hair band was not there. "Luca, what did you do with my hair band?"

"I didn't see it."

"Oh no." She started scanning the ground. It had been there when she woke up. "I'll be back. Walter, why don't you take them for barbecue."

She ran for the shed. Was Gaian still scrying for her? Had he seen Mr. Felix? He'd probably given up, but she didn't want Mr. Felix to get in trouble or involved.

Inside the shed everything looked just like they'd left it. Even the two empty plates were still there. She searched her bed, then looked under the cot. There it was.

"What's so special about that hair band?" Brayton asked behind her.

"It's spelled to prevent the witches from finding me," she said, slipping it on the end of her braid.

Brayton shut the door behind him and leaned on the wall again with his arms crossed. "You told that man you were a witch."

"No, I didn't."

"Yes, you did, yet I couldn't detect your lie. Why is that Honey?"

Darn him. They'd been getting along so well. "I don't know Brayton, maybe because I wasn't intending to deceive him and the words just came out wrong."

He pushed off the wall and approached her, sniffing. "You smell like a witch, but you smell like a wolf too."

"I washed these clothes in a witch's house."

"You're a curse breaker."

He was so close now she had to tilt her head back to see his face. "You knew that already."

"Curse breakers are witches."

She shook her head. "I don't think they are, and I think I know why I'm the first one in over a hundred years."

"Why?"

"Because of my parents."

He put his hands on her shoulders. "What about them Honey?"

"I can't tell you Brayton."

"Honey, I'm your friend and your future alpha. You can tell me anything."

He was so close all she could smell was his body spray. She wouldn't say it was her favorite smell, but she did like it.

"You feel it too, don't you?" His voice had a breathy, raspy sound to it that wasn't quite a whisper.

"Feel what?"

"When we're standing this close, don't you feel like, I don't know, you want to hug me or something?" She must have imagined there was a rasp in his voice. It sounded completely normal now.

"Do you want a hug? I thought you were mad at me."

He shook his head. "I'm not mad. Confused, sad, glad you're here, but not mad."

She studied his blue-gray eyes. He did look like what he said. "Why are you sad?"

"Because you won't confide in me."

"Why are you confused?"

"Because I should be mad but all I want to do is protect you and be with you, but you don't seem to feel the same way."

He truly sounded hurt. She put her hand over one of the ones on her shoulder. "If you were in danger Brayton, I would protect you."

"But you don't want to be with me?"

"I'm here with you now, aren't I?"

"You didn't choose to be here with me though. I invited myself."

"I don't mind. We should probably go find everyone else though. You want some barbecue?" She stepped away from him to retrieve the two paper plates on the box.

The door slammed open. "Brayton Mooney, what are you doing in here alone with my daughter?"

"Your daughter?"

Bio-dad stepped in and glared at him. "She's as good as."

"We were talking and were about to leave so I could throw these away." Honey lifted the plates in her hands.

Alpha Silver scrutinized both of them, then stepped back, giving her a clear path to the open door. "Go ahead, Honey. Brayton and I need to have a little chat."

She found the rest of her friends sitting on folding chairs at a make-shift table made of wooden planks across some old sawhorses. Frederica was bouncing Mika on her knee with Luca hovering close by. Mr. Felix was on her other side and Walter was next to him. Honey sat down across from Frederica.

"How is it?"

"Delicious," Mr. Felix said. "It's true, wolves are kings of the barbecue."

"And queens," his daughter said.

"Yes, and queens."

"I think you can tell your wife her vision came true and it wasn't what she suspected," Honey said, nodding at Luca.

"Oh, believe me, I will," Mr. Felix said, "and before you run off again, here."

He handed her a small spiral shell.

"That's pretty. You're not using acorns anymore?"

"I ran out. I have to wait for fall and collect more this time."

"Mom thinks he's silly for using them," Frederica informed Honey.

"There's nothing silly about it. Using natural materials is good for the environment. Consider a metal charm. The metal has to be dug up and melted, both which take a lot of energy. An acorn, however, needs only to be picked up and easily lasts as long as the spell does, as long as there isn't a worm. You have to be careful about that or the portal might expire early."

"Don't the oils in the acorn go rancid eventually?" Honey asked, thinking of some of the essential oils her mom always made sure were fresh to avoid the same problem.

"It doesn't appear to affect the portals. I've tested acorns that have been stored under various conditions, including in my pocket for a year."

"And through the washer several times," Frederica snickered. "He left a pile of them on the back porch and a squirrel broke in and stole them. The squirrel figured out how to portal into the bird feeder. Mom was not happy."

"A portalling squirrel? I not realize non-vitches kould use portals. How much does one kost?" Alpha Henry asked from the other end of the planks.

"Portalling squirrels are free, but you have to catch them yourself," Mr. Felix snarked. "Portals, on the other hand, are a thousand each, but it's worth it if you consider how quickly you can get from one location to another, and it's good for multiple people, as many as you want in the ten seconds it's open."

"Ha, funny. I vill pass on squirrel, but portal zounds like a good deal. Ve should talk."

"Mmm, sure."

29

BRAYTON

Alpha Silver shut the door behind Honey so that it was just him and Brayton in the shed. It reminded Brayton strongly of being sent to the principal's office except for the shed part.

Alpha Silver crossed his arms and pinned him with a sharp gaze. "Okay, Brayton, tell me what's going on."

"What are you talking about?"

"You're acting weird, even for a teenager. In fact, I'd say you have a serious crush on Honey."

"It's not a crush."

"What is it then?"

He really didn't know Alpha Silver well, and after the way Honey had just basically shut him down, he wasn't in the mood to talk.

"I don't know. Stupidity."

"And she doesn't return your affections?"

"No."

Alpha Silver walked across the small room and sat on the cot where Honey had slept. "She is pretty amazing isn't she."

"Yeah."

"My brother did a good job. I still can't believe how well he hid her from everyone."

Maybe he could get some answers from Alpha Silver. "Did you ever meet Honey's mom?"

Alpha Silver focused on Brayton instead of the wall he'd been staring at. "I did, although that was before Honey was born, of course."

"What pack was she from?"

Alpha Silver shook his head and stood up. "It doesn't matter. Look, I know you like her, but she's very young and she's got a lot of things going on. "I suggest you forget about her. I'll do what I should have done in the first place and take her into my pack."

"Mom really likes having Honey around."

"Honey hasn't been around all that much, and she likely won't be able to return to school either. Just put her out of your mind, Brayton, and live your life."

He sounded so final, like Brayton would never see his beautiful, smart, wonderful Honey again. That was the problem though, wasn't it? She wasn't really his. Whatever he was feeling couldn't be the mating bond because she didn't feel it back. Maybe he broke it when he stabbed her in the heart or maybe she wasn't his fated mate at all. It seemed like every guy she met was ready to fall at her feet. He'd been so sure though ever since that fateful day in the library when he caught her scent outside the bathroom and suddenly *knew*. He could remember it like it was yesterday even now. On top of that, it explained why he'd lost all interest in dating other girls after he met her and even why he was so determined to collect her for his mom when he discovered her in that soup kitchen.

Inside he was screaming and thrashing and felt like pummeling something, but he made sure Alpha Silver didn't see. "Yeah, I'll do that. Good talk."

He barely suppressed a growl when Alpha Silver's hand fell on his shoulder. "Brayton, what are you, nineteen now? There are literally thousands of other girls out there you haven't met yet. You're too young to tie yourself down to one yet."

"Sure," he managed to grunt.

Alpha Silver patted his shoulder, then thankfully released him. "Come on, let's go eat before all the food is gone. Those Russian wolves can really pack it away."

"That's all right. You go. I'm not hungry. I think I'll go for a run."

His mom would have argued with him, but Alpha Silver just nodded with irritating understanding, "Well, you're in a great place for it. I'll send one of my guards with you. Be careful."

"I will."

Brayton walked to the back edge of the property to strip and transform. The guard was already in wolf form when he joined him. Brayton caught a whiff of magic and of Honey when he left the property that made him want to howl his pain, but he held it in. No point in embarrassing himself any further.

A few feet from the border he found an animal trail that skirted the property and led into Yellowstone. Could animals sense the curse too? More than animals had used the trail though, and recently. He smelled several human wolves from different packs, spying no doubt. Had they seen the way Honey had sprinted around the border and then killed the ghost, or whatever it was? She was amazing.

He ran past bear and buffalo and elk, through sulfurous-smelling steam, over rocks and trees, and through a cold, crystal clear creek. The stark beauty calmed him, yet at the same time, he wished Honey was there. She'd probably want to explore everything or maybe she'd race him.

What had she meant about curse breakers not being witches and what was she hiding?

She was always hiding things. It had taken her months to tell everyone her age and she still transformed in private. What could her parents have done to make her a curse breaker? Had they conceived with the help of magic perhaps?

She'd told the portal witch that a witch had killed her mom because she married her dad. Why would a witch care who a wolf married? Had her mom been a prisoner? That would explain why she hid for so long and why Alpha Silver's brother helped her.

Wait, what if, could Honey be the witch's daughter? Maybe the weirdo had forced himself on Honey's mom.

All the seemingly disparate clues in his head rearranged themselves to point at one shining truth.

Honey was both wolf and witch.

It explained everything – the magic, why she was so friendly with the witches, her ability to break curses, and her lack of ability to talk in wolf form.

But how? She was supposed to be cursed. Her parents were supposed to be cursed. Oh. Curse breaker. That's how she knew.

That's what she was hiding from him.

Honey was a hybrid.

A loose branch appeared out of nowhere and sent him flying over a large lichen-covered boulder to the not-so-thick grass at the bottom of it. Instead of getting back on his feet, he laid his head back and stared up at the clear blue sky. Honey was a hybrid. That meant…she had to die.

His view of the sky was interrupted by the head of Alpha Silver's guard staring down at him from the top of the boulder. The guard barked an inquiry, probably concerned that Brayton wasn't moving. Brayton rolled to his feet and gave himself a good shake.

He was wrong. Honey couldn't be a hybrid. She was too good a wolf. Sure, her wolf was a little smaller than normal, but it wasn't completely outside of the norm. She could certainly run and climb and do everything else wolves could, actually a lot better than most wolves. She was smart and loyal, at least to the Little boys.

Wolves couldn't break curses though.

Nor could witches, at least none in the past hundred years or so. Was the curse the reason? What if curse breakers were hybrids, not all of course, but some small percentage? If all hybrids were killed at birth, no wonder there were no curse breakers.

He rejoined the guard on the original trail. The guard indicated they should go back, but Brayton wasn't ready to return yet. He started jogging in the opposite direction.

Honey was…wow. She was so much more special than he'd realized. If anyone found out she was a hybrid though…if his own dad found out, by law he'd have to kill her or turn her in for others to kill. No wonder she felt like she couldn't be herself.

In any event, if he was right, if Honey was a hybrid, this attraction, this need to be near her, he had to let it go. He was years from being the alpha of his pack, but he couldn't afford to get tangled up with her any more than he already was. He didn't wish her any harm, but he had to think of the future. Someday he'd need a mate, a full-blooded wolf, to be the Luna of his pack and he knew he wouldn't be able to settle for someone if he allowed his attraction for Honey to get any stronger.

His heart felt like it was literally being torn in two. It was for the best, but…Alpha Silver was right. Did he know what she was? He must. Why had Honey told Alpha Silver but not him? He wasn't her alpha. It wasn't fair. No. It didn't matter. He had to let her go and live his life. He was being ridiculous. He hadn't even known her for a year. He'd just pretend he'd never met her. Honey who?

How long had he been sitting on the path staring at a tree in the dark? Alpha Silver's guard probably thought he was nuts. Running wasn't helping and now he was tired. He stood and headed back the way they'd come. Faint booms from distant fireworks added a low rumble to the night noises in the park. Somewhere a wolf howled. Brayton didn't howl back. If he howled all the wolves within range would hear his pain. She might hear and then she'd ask him what was wrong with those big green earnest eyes of hers and he'd fall apart.

Gads he wanted her to smile at him and hug him like she did her friends, just once.

No. He'd never be able to let her go.

More wolves had been by since he left, but they appeared to be following the trail around the property and not trying to go in. Instead of going back to get his clothes, he turned toward the entrance to follow the trail. What he needed was a good fight, something to get his mind off Honey. Maybe someone would be foolish enough to challenge him.

The trail followed the edge of the property, then split to head toward Yellowstone or across the road. Brayton followed the trail that crossed the road. Maybe he'd find some wolves watching from there to challenge.

On the other side of the road, the trail headed uphill to weave behind and between trees and rocks, creating plenty of places to spy on Honey's land. Almost directly across from the entrance, he finally caught a whiff of something fresh that absolutely shouldn't be there – a witch, male. The witch was above them on the slope somewhere. Brayton turned around and jogged back a few hundred yards, then worked his way up so he could come down on top of his prey. His guard spotted the witch first and nudged Brayton. It couldn't be any more obvious as to what the witch was doing considering he was lying on his belly on top of a large, embedded boulder with a pair of binoculars trained towards Honey's property.

The smart thing to do would be to retrieve his clothes and dress before confronting the witch. His guard had no doubt already sent a telepathic message to inform Alpha Silver of the situation. He could just let him take care of it. Brayton didn't want to do the smart thing though. He wanted a fight, or at least to chase something. Yes, chasing a witch down the steep slope was exactly what he needed.

He barked, then growled when the man turned to look over his shoulder.

"I have as much right to be here as you do wolf," the witch said.

Brayton shook his head, then touched his eyes with his paw.

"You don't like my binoculars? Oh, are you a member of that pack? Perfect." The man sat up to face Brayton and stuck his hand into the top of his own shirt. Brayton heard the faint chink of metal. How many necklaces was the man wearing?

"Change," the man abruptly ordered.

A force like alpha power but weaker tried to force Brayton to obey. He easily shrugged it off. He caught a hint of magic that reminded him of Honey and the guard next to him growled.

"I said transform!" the man tried again.

No way was Brayton going to obey him even if it would make it easier to communicate. He growled and jerked his head to the side, clearly indicating the man should leave.

The man's hand moved under his shirt. "Something a little stronger then. Transform!"

Brayton's body started changing and there was nothing he could do to stop it. The guard, still in wolf form, stepped between Brayton and the witch but it didn't stop the transformation.

"Move it, mutt," the witch commanded.

The guard growled and sat defiantly where he was. How was the guard able to resist when he couldn't? Brayton caught another whiff of Honey's magic. Her charms. The guard must be wearing his. She hadn't bought them, Brayton realized, she'd made them herself and they worked well. He should have worn his.

His forced transformation finished. Brayton stayed in a squat both to use the guard as a shield and because he had no wish to expose himself to a peeping witch. "Why are you spying on the property, witch?"

"I'm asking the questions here. Is Honey Smith present on the property?"

"Who is Honey Smith?"

The man touched something inside his shirt again. "Answer me! Yes or no?"

Brayton couldn't stop himself, so he didn't. "Yes or no."

"Say one or the other!" the man nearly shouted.

Ha. "One or the other." He sure hoped Alpha Silver was coming soon.

"Nod if Honey Smith is present on the property," the man commanded smugly.

Brayton tried, he really tried to shake his head first, but whatever magic the witch was using made it impossible.

"Thank you. That's all I wanted to know. Now depart this world." The witch flung something at him. The guard leaped up and intercepted it with his body. His body lit up with a red light and again Brayton smelled Honey's magic, but this time it smelled like burnt sugar. The guard dropped hard on the ground, making no attempt to land. He looked – dead.

Brayton had never seen anyone die before. Later, he would scold himself for not attacking or running, but in the moment, he simply asked, "Why did you do that?"

"I said, depart this world."

Brayton rolled to the side to avoid whatever the witch had just flung at him, then threw himself at the man before he had a chance to grab anything else. The man put one hand out and Brayton's vision was abruptly filled with a brilliant light, then intense pain. He fell to the ground, instinctively curling into a ball to protect his face from any more damage. He couldn't protect the rest of him though.

"The other way would have been easier," he thought he heard the man say over the roar of the fire in his ears.

"No!" That was Honey's voice.

The heat stopped. He heard the very recognizable sound of fist meeting its target, then a few moments later, a soft voice right above him, "Oh, Brayton."

He wanted to see her but he couldn't open his eyes. "Honey." His voice sounded like he felt, cracked and burnt.

"We'll get you to Dr. Ziga. Liam, Luca, you grab Brayton. I'm opening a portal in that stone right there. Someone get the guard."

"Witch killed him," Brayton pushed out just before two sets of hands went under him and lifted his body. "Spell."

"He's alive, Brayton. Here."

The worst of his pain suddenly vanished. "That will get you through the portal. Get better Brayton."

They were carrying him away. "Wait. Honey, I need to tell you."

"There's no time."

"Wait."

They weren't stopping.

"I know Honey, and I don't care," he yelled.

30

RECKONING

"I know Honey, and…"

What did he know? Did he know what she was? If he survived, maybe she could ask him later. He didn't look good. All the skin she'd been able to see was burned black and red, and his face… She wanted to cry, but she didn't have that luxury, not yet. The guard carrying his unconscious friend stepped into the portal. She wanted with everything she had to follow too, but she had to make sure Gaian Graves never harmed anyone else again.

She tossed the shell through the portal to close it, then turned to face the awful man still lying prone on the ground where she'd knocked him out both with a punch and with her magic. Zavier had his phone out and was shining it in the man's face.

"Do you know who it is?" he asked.

"Gaian Graves, the man who murdered my parents."

"This is the man who murdered Matt?" Alpha Silver asked.

"Yes."

Her bio-dad let out an awful growl and lunged toward Gaian. Honey stepped in his way at the same time Zavier grabbed Alpha Silver's arm.

"No. You can't kill him. It will get you in trouble with the witches. I have a better plan." She wished she'd thought of it the first time she'd had Gaian under her power, but she hadn't known enough magic then. She squatted and checked his neck. Yep, loaded with charms and the chains were spelled to prevent breaking and removal. He had learned from their last interaction. With a quick thought, she removed the preventive spells and pulled the charms over his head, then tossed them to the side. "If he's smart, he probably has other charms hidden on his body. The easiest way to be sure they're gone is to strip him, perhaps with claws?" she glanced at Alpha Silver.

"I can take care of that," he said with a gleam in his eye.

Gaian moaned.

"Better hurry," Honey said, squatting behind Gaian's head and holding his arms out so he couldn't touch anything. Alpha Silver extended his fingers and partially transformed them into claws which he swiped down Gaian's front. Within seconds, Gaian's clothes were sliced and ripped from his torso and every limb.

Honey slapped his face and stood. "Wake up."

"What? What have you done to me?"

"Stand up," Honey ordered.

"Where are my clothes?"

"You're lying on them. Stand up."

Alpha Silver's guard grabbed Gaian's wrist and jerked him upright. The bright light from Zavier's phone and the chill in the air did nothing for Gaian's pale, naked body. Honey pretended she was looking at a plucked chicken instead of a disgusting older man.

"Like what you see?" Gaian sneered as she walked around him.

"No. Nice tattoo though." Zavier helpfully focused on the dark shield shape in the middle of Gaian's back. With her magic sight, she could see a faint glow encasing Gaian's body – a protection spell based on the smell. She focused on the molecules forming the spell and scattered them. The glow vanished.

"What are you going to do," Alpha Silver asked when Honey had finished her inspection.

"Yeah, what are you going to do," Gaian smirked. "You realize any aggressive act will not only prove your instability, but it might very well start a war between the witches and the wolves. That will be all the more reason to put you down, and you can't tell anyone who killed the guard and injured that boy because if you do, I'll tell them about you."

She froze his tongue.

"Is the tattoo new?"

He opened his mouth and nothing came out. Good, she'd found all the charms.

"You might want to get your money back. Gaian Graves, you killed my parents with your power and you attempted to kill a third person, an innocent person, using your power tonight. I cannot allow you to do that ever again." She imagined the core of fire she sensed in him being placed in a sealed, metal bucket, then imagined a strong, fireproof rope wrapping around him to hold any other fire tightly inside. She tied it with a strong knot behind his neck. "I have bound your powers. If you behave, I might someday remove the binding. If you tell anyone about me though, and I am killed, it will never be removed." She touched the back of his neck and imagined a second knot anchoring itself to the first and disappearing into the nether. That should keep it in place. She walked around to face him again. "It can only be removed by a curse breaker and I am the only one."

"Liar," he said when his tongue unfroze.

"Try it."

Gaian put his hand over the hand of the guard holding him in place. Gaian's defiant glare turned to surprise, then disbelief. It flashed to panic, then turned almost smug. "Nice trick. I'm sure whoever sold you the charm will be able to undo it."

"What about Noah? He should be punished for hurting him too," Alpha Silver's remaining guard said.

"You're right," Honey said. Hopefully this meant her dad's remaining guard wouldn't report her for using magic, or maybe he'd think she was using charms like Gaian did. She pictured what she wanted in her head then touched the top of Gaian's head to set the reverse shield in place. "For every charm you use that's meant to harm or control another person, the action will instead be cast upon you and no shield charm will be able to protect you."

"You can't do that."

"Why not? Would you like to test it? I can give you one of those killing curses to try it with."

263

"Killing curses?" Zavier said.

"Yeah, I'm pretty sure that's what that smell is. Can I borrow your light?"

"Use mine," Alpha Silver said, handing Honey his phone.

She scanned the ground where the guard had been lying. Nothing stood out to her until she switched to her other sight. A lone pebble on the ground between Gaian and where the guard had fallen glowed a faint purple-black.

"There," she pointed, "but don't touch it if you want to keep it for evidence." She sniffed. "There's another one somewhere."

She followed her nose. The second pebble lay several feet past the first one and was glowing a bright blue-purple. "This one is still active." She looked back at Gaian. "How do you deactivate this?"

"Touch it and find out."

"I'll pass." She'd read about them once. Almost all the branches of magic could make spells to kill but the most deadly and effective ones came from necromancers. Their spells could rip a person's soul right from their body, leaving the body unharmed and human investigators unable to explain why a person died. Knowing Gaian, that's what this was.

She squatted to study it. The pebble was lying on moss, so just touching it with something living wasn't enough.

"Leave it, Witch. We can cover it and let the enforcers take care of it," Alpha Silver said.

"You're going to call the enforcers?"

"Per the treaty, any witch or wolf accused of a crime by the other side has the right to a trial."

"But then…."

"I know," her bio-dad cut her off.

"And you guys could…"

"Little witch, thank you for your assistance, but we will handle it from here," her bio-dad said firmly, telling her with his eyes to play along. What was he up to?

"She's not a witch! She's a monster," Gaian exclaimed.

"What, because she bound your powers?" her bio-dad snorted. "Naked man, I hereby arrest you for using magic to force your will on wolves and for the attempted murders of Noah Rush and Brayton Mooney who confronted you when they caught you spying on Alpha Zavier's pack. I'm sorry to say the bank is not going to get the land back this time."

"The bank?"

"Or were you hoping to somehow acquire the land for yourself now that the curse is gone."

"What are you talking about?"

"Playing dumb are you? Who do you work for?"

"No one."

"Who told you about the curse?"

"What curse?"

"You admit you are just here to spy on the wolves then?"

"Not the wolves – her." Gaian nodded at Honey.

Bio-dad looked between Gaian and her with a disgusted look. "That's despicable. She's barely half your age, if that."

"What? You think…" Gaian released a loud, high-pitched sound that might have been a laugh. "Unlike you wolves we think about more than our next lay. She's a hybrid, the child of a wolf and a witch. She's a monster. I'm here to capture her and bring her to justice."

Alpha Silver made a show of looking her up and down and sniffing at her. "She doesn't look like a hybrid, nor does she smell like one. If she was half wolf, I'd smell wolf. I smell magic."

Honey got the hint and quickly pulled up her air shield. Behind her back, she pulled her grandmother's charm from the nether and held it tightly in her hand. Pretending to be all witch probably wouldn't protect her once Gaian told his story to the Enforcers, but pretending she was a witch and that they didn't know her might protect Alpha Zavier and her bio-dad.

"Lie all you want, a blood test will tell the truth."

"Her blood is not the issue. You attempted to kill two people who caught you spying on wolf land. The evidence is indisputable. Alpha Zavier, did you contact the enforcers?"

"A call has been placed."

"Good. Make sure you show them the killing charms. I'll go check on Brayton and Noah and contact the enforcers on that end if they haven't already been contacted." He turned to Honey. "Miss, would you like to come with me? We might need your expertise."

He knew she wasn't a healer, but her bio-dad gave a discrete little nod, so she said, "Of course."

"You can run all you want," Gaian smirked, "but once Madame Wixx announces you exist, your days are numbered."

"Who is this Madame Wixx? Is that who you work for?" Bio-dad demanded.

Gaian thrust his nose in the air. "She is the head of the greatest founding family still in existence. I am like a son to her."

"Why would she care about this little witch?" Alpha Silver asked.

"Because she is a hybrid, a curse on all of us. As long as she lives, we cannot thrive."

"If the girl was a hybrid and this Madame Wixx already knew about her, then wouldn't she have already told the world?" Zavier quizzed. "If she is truly the head of a family she knows the law."

"She has her reasons."

Bio-dad nodded. "I bet she doesn't know of this girl at all, does she? I bet you wanted her for yourself, if not because you are attracted to her, then perhaps…her power? You wanted to use her, didn't you?"

"What power?" Gaian scoffed.

Honey didn't need her nose to tell her Gaian was hiding something.

"She just bound your powers and put a powerful spell on you despite all the charms and the tattoo you protected yourself with. She's clearly more powerful that you." Bio-dad squinted at Gaian. "Not only did you attempt to kill two wolves, you had plans to capture and enslave a witch."

"You can make all the claims you want, but it doesn't change what she is. As soon as the enforcers test her they'll set me free."

"You claimed self-defense yet there's not a scratch on you and an alpha's only son and the man guarding him are both in the hospital, not to mention, death charms are illegal. You aren't going free, no matter what your excuse." Bio-dad leaned closer to Gaian and sniffed. "You know wolves can smell when you lie and when you're nervous and afraid, right? You don't smell so good."

"Alpha Silver, the enforcers will be here shortly," Zavier said, tapping his screen.

"Good. Can you handle it from here? I need to check on the Mooney boy and let his parents know what happened. Tell the enforcers I'll give my statement back home. Alden," Alpha Silver said to the guard still holding Gaian, "can you pack up once you're done here and fly back with everyone's things?"

"You know if you leave the binding on me, the witches will know about you. They'll be able to detect and recognize your magic," Gaian smirked. "There won't be anywhere you can hide."

He was right, she realized with a sinking heart, and they'd probably be able to tie her to the library break-in too. Phooey.

"Ignore him," Alpha Silver said, holding out his hand toward Honey. "My free portal trial. Take me to the boy."

Honey took the small shell Alpha Silver was offering and pictured a blank wall in Dr. Ziga's practice again. "It's ready. Goodbye Alpha Zavier."

Zavier thrust out his hand. She was sure he would have hugged her if Gaian hadn't been there. "Goodbye, little witch. Thank you, for everything, and good luck."

NOTES FROM THE AUTHOR

Sorry for the cliff-hanger. Not trying to be evil. I wrote the series with no goals as to how many books I was aiming for, then chopped it into publishable pieces. There are three more pieces after this. They're already written and nearly ready to be published so if they aren't online yet, they should be shortly. They only get more exciting from here.

Reader feedback is very much appreciated. Please leave a review if you liked the story and tell your friends and your librarian. (That's me marketing. Impressive, right?)

You may have noticed the 'Clean Fiction' logo at the beginning of the book. I love to read but sometimes, okay often, find myself in the middle of a good story and abruptly I'm in someone's bedroom getting a play-by-play. Sex happens but I don't need to be there. I'm not the only one who feels this way. I discovered whole communities on social media and a magazine devoted to clean reads. To make it easier for like-minded people to find clean books and to encourage other authors to go clean, I thought a logo on said books would be helpful. So, if you are a writer or know one and would like a copy of the logo, drop me a line. LisaL.author@gmail.com. I'd be glad to share. I have both gold-foil and black-ink versions, or you can design your own.